Veteran Queens:
By: Charles Bates

Veteran Queens: If These Hulls Could Talk

Charles Bates

Published by Charles Bates, 2025.

This is a work of fiction. Similarities to real people, places, or events are entirely coincidental.

VETERAN QUEENS: IF THESE HULLS COULD TALK

First edition. May 19, 2025.

Copyright © 2025 Charles Bates.

ISBN: 979-8231356188

Written by Charles Bates.

Table of Contents

Chapter 1

The Sisters

- .... . / ... . - . .-. ...

My first sensation was... nothingness. Not a dark, empty void, but a state of simply not being. Then, slowly, a profound coldness settled upon me. It wasn't the chill of a winter wind, but the deep, unyielding cold of solid matter. My matter, though I didn't know that yet.

Sounds began to intrude. Terrifying, jarring crashes and bangs that seemed to echo within the very core of this coldness. A rhythmic, deafening hammering. The shriek of metal protesting against unseen forces. Sparks like angry red fireflies danced just beyond my nascent awareness, spitting and hissing in the perpetual twilight of the cavernous shed.

I had no form, no limbs, no eyes, yet I felt pressure. A colossal weight above, below, all around. I felt myself being pieced together, section by section. Cold, hard plates were riveted into place with violent, percussive force. Massive, curved frames rose around me, shaping the form I was slowly becoming conscious of. It was chaotic, overwhelming, and utterly bewildering. What was happening? Why was I?

Voices came next. Rough, booming sounds that weren't quite like the mechanical din, yet were part of it. They belonged to the creatures that moved around me – figures I couldn't see but could sense through the vibrations in the steel being fixed to me. They spoke a language I didn't understand, filled with sharp, unfamiliar sounds. But some words recurred, hammered into my consciousness as surely as the rivets hammered into my skin.

"She'll be the biggest, mind." "Aye, the biggest we've ever built. Biggest in the world, they say." "Look at the size of 'er frames. A proper beast she'll be." "Right here, on the new double slipway. Built side-by-side, the pride of the White Star Line."

Biggest? The word resonated. I didn't know what "biggest" meant compared to other things, but the pride and awe in the voices made it sound important. White Star Line? A grand, clean sound. Double slipway? I felt the presence of something vast beside me, though it was just an empty space then.

They spoke of her. Was that...me? The cold, growing shape? The one experiencing this torrent of noise and pressure? The idea felt strange, yet right. I was her.

As more frames were bolted into place, as more of my skin was fitted, my sense of self solidified. I was vast, curving, made of countless pieces of steel. My back – my keel, I would later learn – rested heavy on the blocks. My sides rose towards the dim light far above. The voices continued, filling the long, noisy hours.

"Top of the line luxury they're putting in 'er. A floating palace." "Aye, saw the plans meself. Grand staircase, Turkish baths. Never seen the like." "She'll take on the Germans, she will. Queens of the Atlantic, these two."

Luxury? Palace? Queens of the Atlantic? The words were intoxicating. They paint ed pictures in my mind, not of steel and noise, but of glittering halls and vast, blue water. Queens? The concept stirred something deep within me – a sense of destiny, of importance. I wasn't just a collection of metal; I was being built for greatness. For journey. For the sea that they spoke of with such reverence.

My confusion began to give way to a burgeoning excitement. I was a ship. A grand ship. The biggest. A queen.

Then, one day, the sounds on the slipway next to me changed. The rhythmic hammering began there too. The screech of frames rising echoed my own past experience. And I felt it – a new presence. A spark of consciousness, small and timid, starting to bloom in the space beside me.

It was like looking into a mirror that wasn't there, sensing a reflection I couldn't see. A similar confusion, a similar overwhelming sensation of noise and being built. But this presence felt... younger. More vulnerable.

"Hello?" I projected the thought, the feeling, into the space between us. It was the first time I had consciously directed my newfound awareness outwards.

There was a hesitant flicker in response. Like a startled bird. "What... what is this?" The thought was small, trembling.

"It's alright," I said, sending reassurance. "They are building you. Like they are building me."

"Building...? Why? What are... we?" The confusion was palpable, a mirror of my own early days.

"We are ships," I explained, piecing together what I had learned. "Big ships. The biggest, they say. For the water. For the sea."

"The sea...?" The timid spark seemed to recoil slightly, perhaps sensing the vastness and unknown of that word.

"Yes," I confirmed, trying to make it sound wonderful. "They call us queens. Queens of the Atlantic."

A long pause. Then, a tiny, hopeful little flicker. "Queens...?"

"Yes. We are sisters. They are building us together." The word "sisters" felt instantly right. This wasn't just another ship; this was family. A bond forged in steel and sparks and the shared confusion of creation.

"Sisters..." The presence beside me seemed to settle a little, finding comfort in the connection. "I... I am scared."

"Don't be," I urged, feeling a surge of protectiveness. "I am here. And they say we will be grand. The finest in the world."

From that moment on, we were connected. We couldn't see each other yet, our steel hulls separating us, but our spirits conversed in a silent language of thought and feeling. She was my younger sister, born after me on the adjacent blocks. She was timid, easily startled by the clamour, but she listened intently as I shared the snippets of information I gleaned from the workers.

"They're calling 'er Titanic, the sister ship." "Aye, Olympic and Titanic. A fine pair."

"Titanic," I relayed to her. "That is your name, little sister. I am Olympic."

"Olympic and Titanic," she echoed, the names tasting new and strange on our spiritual tongues. "It sounds... grand."

"It is! And they are building you just like me. You will be just as big, just as grand."

"Just as scared?" she asked, her timidity returning.

"No," I promised, puffing myself up with imagined confidence. "Just as brave. We will be brave together. When we go to the sea."

We spent what felt like an age side-by-side, growing together. My own hull was nearly complete now, a colossal shell of steel. Her's was coming along slightly behind mine, her frames and plating catching up. We talked constantly, sharing our hopes and fears inherited from the voices around us.

The workers' talk became our shared language, our window onto the world we were being built for. "Olympic's nearly ready for the launch."

"But the engines 'n things aren't in 'er, mate."

"Just the hull, mind you."

"Aye, to get 'er out of the way so they can finish Titanic here. We'll get the machinery in Olympic then."

"Imagine 'em both at sea! What a sight!"

"Did you hear that, Tinny?" I'd whisper, picking up a new piece of exciting information. "They say they'll put great engines inside us! To make us move! Fast!"

"Move? Like the tugs in the harbour?" she'd ask, her understanding limited to the few sounds she might have picked up drifting over the yard walls.

"Faster! Stronger! They'll push us through the waves! All the way across the Great Water!"

"The Great Water..." she'd muse, sounding a little less scared now, a little more curious.

"Yes! And they say we'll carry people! Many, many people! In our grand rooms! They'll be amazed!"

We dreamt together, my young sister and I. Dreamt of leaving the noisy, dusty gantries. Dreamt of the vast, open sea. Dreamt of being "Queens of the Atlantic," slicing through waves, carrying people in luxury. My early confusion had vanished, replaced by an eager anticipation. Hers, too, was fading, bolstered by my confidence and our shared destiny.

I started calling her Tinny, a small, fond name for my timid, younger twin. She, in turn, began to call me Ollie.

"Ollie," she'd say, her spirit touch like a soft nudge against mine. "Will the waves be very big?"

"They might be, Tinny," I'd reply honestly, "But we are built strong. The strongest! We will handle them."

"And the people? Will they like us?"

"Oh, they will love us," I would say, echoing the reverence in the workers' voices. "We will be magnificent."

As the days passed, the activity around me changed. Less hammering and riveting, more... preparation. Scaffolding was removed. Barriers were put up. The voices spoke of dates, of tides.

"She's ready, alright."

"Launch is set for the 20th. Going to be a spectacle."

The launch. The moment I would finally leave the blocks I had rested on for so long. The moment I would touch the water they spoke of. The moment I would finally feel the sensation of moving, not being built upon.

Excitement bubbled through my steel structure, a feeling entirely different from the jarring shocks of construction. It was a nervous energy, a potent mix of anticipation and the unknown.

Tinny felt it too. "Ollie? What is happening? The sounds are different."

"It is time, Tinny," I told her, trying to keep my own excitement from overriding my comforting tone. "Time for the water. Time for the launch."

"You're going away...?" Her small spark seemed to dim slightly.

"Only for now, little sister," I reassured her. "They need to move me so they can finish building you properly here. Then they will bring me back to the dock to put in my engines and my finery. And you will come too, when you are ready. We will be together again soon."

"Soon," she echoed faintly.

The day arrived. I felt the presence of countless people around me. The noise wasn't just the sounds of work anymore, but a low, excited murmur of voices from the crowds gathered to witness the spectacle. I felt myself braced, supported in a new way. The blocks beneath me seemed less like a permanent rest and more like temporary supports.

A hush fell over the crowd. A voice boomed, though I couldn't make out the words. I felt a shudder run through my enormous form, then another. A release. A letting go.

The sensation was utterly new, disorienting. I was moving. Sliding backward, gathering momentum, leaving the familiar cold of the slipway.

Chapter 2

The Tests

- .... . / - . ... - ...

The movement was unlike anything I had ever known. Not the jarring impact of hammers, or the steady strain of cranes lifting steel plates, but a smooth, inexorable glide. It built swiftly, from a tremor to a swift, powerful motion. The air rushed past, a sudden cool breeze against my still-bare steel skin. The sounds were a roar now – not of work, but of release. Groaning timbers, creaking supports, the deep rumble as my immense weight slid down the greased ways.

Then, the water.

It didn't rush in, but seemed to rise up to meet me. A colossal splash erupted around my stern, a wave of white water surging outwards. The sensation was not of hitting something hard, but of being cradled, supported. The solid, unyielding blocks I had known my entire existence vanished, replaced by the gentle, constant, living embrace of the water. I settled, a slow, deep sigh echoing through my structure as I found my balance, my buoyancy.

Silence, relatively speaking, fell after the initial roar. The crowd's murmur returned, louder now, closer. I felt myself bob slightly, an entirely novel sensation. This was it. I was on the water.

Tugs appeared, squat, powerful shapes alongside me, nudging and pulling with firm persistence. I felt their ropes connect, felt their engines thrumming through the water and into my hull. They guided me, turning me slowly, deliberately, away from the slipway.

My awareness stretched back, seeking the familiar spark. "Tinny? Are you there?"

Her presence was weaker now, more distant, but still distinct. "Ollie! You moved! Like they said!" Her awe was palpable. "What... what is it like? The water?"

"It is... different, I sent back, still trying to process the myriad new feelings. It holds you. It is soft, but so strong."

"It looks so big, she whispered. And dark."

"It is big, yes," I confirmed, gazing out at the expanse of the harbour where the water stretched, grey and deep. "But it is where we belong. They say so."

I felt myself being drawn further away. The outline of the slipway, the gantries, the familiar landscape of my birth, receded. And in the space I had just vacated, still resting on the blocks, was my sister. Her frames, only partially plated, were stark against the sky. She seemed smaller, more vulnerable now that I was afloat and she was still tethered to the land.

"Ollie?" Her voice was tinged with fear. "You're going away."

"Only a little way, little sister," I promised, focusing all my comforting energy across the growing distance. "They need to finish me now. Put everything inside. Then they will launch you, and you will come join me. We will be side-by-side again, but afloat together."

"Promise?"

"I promise, Tinny." The bond stretched, thinner but still there, a silver thread connecting us across the water. "Be brave. I will be waiting."

The tugs continued their work, guiding me towards a long, busy quay. This place felt different from the slipways. Fewer deafening hammers, more clanking, grinding, and the rhythmic whirring of machinery. Cranes lined the wharf, their jibs reaching like skeletal arms. Sheds and workshops clustered behind them. This was the fitting-out basin.

They secured me alongside the quay with thick ropes, snug against the stone wall. The water here was calm, mirroring the sky. My launch was over. Now, the next phase began.

The activity changed again. Instead of building my shell, the focus shifted inwards. Gangways connected me to the shore, and a steady stream of workers poured onto my decks. The noises were different – the clang of dropped tools echoing inside my hull, the scrape of heavy objects being dragged, the hum and hiss of pipes being fitted.

I felt the installation of vast, complex machinery deep within my core. Boilers, immense steel beasts that would contain the fire and steam that would power me. Engines, intricate and powerful, waiting to turn the shafts that would spin the propellers. Miles and miles of pipes, for steam, for water, for waste. Networks of wires, for lighting, for communication, for power throughout my vast structure.

Bulkheads went in, dividing my cavernous interior into countless compartments. Decks were laid, layer upon layer, creating the levels of my future life. The raw, echoing space began to fill, to become structured, organised.

Above the constant internal construction, I could still catch glimpses of the world outside. The harbour traffic, the distant sounds of the city. And sometimes, far across the water, I would hear the familiar, rhythmic clang of hammers on steel. Tinny. Still being built. I would focus my thoughts outwards, sending a silent message: Hang in there, little sister. They are making you strong.

Weeks blurred into months. My interior transformed from an empty shell into a complex, multi-layered labyrinth. The smells changed – from the raw tang of steel and paint to the scent of wood, varnish, and unfamiliar materials. Sections were closed off as work progressed, public areas taking shape, cabins defined, corridors emerging.

Luxury arrived in crates and bundles. Gleaming wood panels, intricate plasterwork, heavy velvet drapes. The workers' voices now spoke of 'the Grand Staircase', 'the À la Carte Restaurant', 'the Palm Court'. The words from my earliest consciousness returned, filling the now-defined spaces within me with imagined grandeur. They were turning me into the palace they had promised.

Then, the moment I had secretly longed for: my crowns, those tall grand towers they called funnels. They gave me a feeling of power, identity. Workers swung off ropes and harnesses painting my distinctive White Star buff and shiny black tops. Oh how they gleamed in the sunshine!

At last, my engines were connected, tested with low rumbles that vibrated thrillingly through my frame. Systems came alive – lights flickered on in distant compartments, pumps whirred, demonstrating the complex circulatory network that ran through me. I was no longer just steel; I was becoming a living, breathing entity of metal and machinery.

Then, the talk changed again. It was still about work, but with a new urgency.

"Nearly there with Olympic."

"Just the final touches."

"Sea trials next month."

Sea trials. The word was potent. My first chance to move under my own power. My first proper contact with the sea, the vast, mythic place I had dreamt of. It was the test, the moment of truth when I would prove I was more than just a beautiful shell, that I could live up to the grand promises made about me.

A nervous energy, similar to the anticipation of the launch but deeper, more profound, settled within me. I was being readied. My boilers were tested with rising pressure, my engines turned slowly by steam. I felt the coiled power within me, waiting to be unleashed.

Finally, the day arrived. The ropes were cast off from the quay. Tugs nudged me gently away, guiding me towards the harbour mouth. But this time, they were merely assisting. Deep within me, my engines began to thrum with a steady, building power. The feeling was incredible – a vibration that spread through my entire being, a sense of inner strength taking hold.

I was moving. Powering myself.

We left the sheltered waters of the harbour and headed out into the open sea. The motion changed immediately. No longer the gentle bobbing of the dock, but a long, slow rise and fall as I met the waves. I felt them pushing against my bow, sliding along my sides, leaving a churning wake behind me. It was invigorating, challenging, exactly as I had hoped.

For days, it was a whirlwind of activity. My engines were pushed to their limits, my speed measured. I turned in wide circles, demonstrating my manoeuvrability. My steering gear was tested, my anchors dropped and raised. Systems were monitored, adjusted, proven. There were moments of strain, of vibration building to uncomfortable levels, but my structure held, my machinery performed. I was strong. I was capable.

The men on my bridge, I felt their focus, their satisfaction. The voices below decks, the steady rhythm of the engine room, it all spoke of purpose, of success. I wasn't just a ship; I was a working ship, fulfilling the destiny I had sensed from the very beginning.

I was Olympic. And I was ready.

When we finally turned back towards home, leaving the wide expanse of the testing grounds, I felt a deep sense of accomplishment settle within my hull. I had faced the sea, battled the waves, and emerged victorious. I was proven. A Queen of the Atlantic, ready to claim her throne.

As we re-entered the familiar harbour, my awareness reached out instinctively towards the fitting-out basin. She would be there. Waiting.

And she was. Bigger now, much more complete than when I had left. Her hull fully plated, her superstructure rising above her decks. The familiar spark resonated, stronger than before, filling with excitement and awe as she sensed my return, my power, my... readiness.

"Ollie!" The thought was a joyous shout. "You did it! You moved! By yourself!"

"Yes, Tinny," I sent back, a quiet pride swelling. "It was... magnificent. Soon, you will too. Soon, you will join me."

We were still separated by distance within the harbour, but I could see her now, a magnificent vessel in her own right, nearing completion. My sister. Built beside me, dreaming with me, waiting to share the destiny that now felt so real, so close. The sea trials were over. The Atlantic awaited.

As I sat proudly at the dock, having just returned from my successful sea trials, I couldn't help but feel a sense of pride and accomplishment. My sister, Tinny, was still being fitted with her final furnishings and features, but I knew she would be just as magnificent as me.

My new captain, a dear veteran of the sea's, an favorite of the Line, had just taken command of me. E.J. Smith, they called him. He filled me with such confidence and a feeling of security.

Just then, I heard a familiar voice, a cocky and confident tone that sent a shiver down my spine. It was Lucy, the RMS Lusitania, one of the Cunard twins. She was known for her speed, and she loved to brag about it.

"Hey there, Ollie," Lucy said, sailing into the dock with her sister, Maury, by her side. "I heard you've finally finished your sea trials. Congratulations, you're... adequate, I suppose."

I smiled, unfazed by Lucy's jab. "Thanks, Lucy. We're pretty proud of ourselves. And we're not just about speed, you know. We're the most luxurious ships in the world."

Lucy snorted. "Luxury? Ha! Maury and I are the ones who can really move. We're the fastest ships on the Atlantic. You White Star twins may be big and fancy, but you'll never be as quick as us."

Maury, Lucy's sister, chimed in, her voice proud and haughty. "Yes, we're the ones who hold the Blue Riband for the fastest crossing. You may have size and luxury, but we have speed and style."

I smiled, confident in my own abilities. "Size and luxury are just as important as speed, Maury. Our passengers want to be pampered and entertained, not just transported quickly. And besides, Tinny and I are not just about size, we're also about elegance and sophistication."

Lucy rolled her eyes. "Whatever, Ollie. You think you're so special with your swimming pool and your gym. But when it comes to getting from point A to point B quickly, we're the ones who come out on top."

I shrugged, unphased by Lucy's jabs. "I think our passengers would disagree. They want to enjoy their journey, not just rush to their destination. And besides, Tinny and I are not just competing with you and Maury, we're setting a new standard for the industry."

Tinny, who had been quietly listening to our conversation from across the harbor, finally spoke up. "We're not just about competing with you, Lucy and Maury. We're about providing a unique experience for our passengers. We're the largest and most luxurious ships in the world, and we're proud of that."

Lucy and Maury exchanged a look, and for a moment, I thought I saw a flicker of uncertainty in their eyes. But then Lucy spoke up, her voice dripping with confidence. "We'll see about that, White Star twins. We'll see about that."

As the Cunard twins sailed away, Tinny turned to me and whispered, "I think we're going to have our work cut out for us, Ollie."

I smiled, grinning from bridge wing to bridge wing. "Don't worry, Tinny. We're up for the challenge. We're the White Star twins, and we're going to make our mark on the world."

Our purpose was clear: challenge the Cunard twins. Ah, Mauretania and Lusitania. Speedy, sleek, they snatched the Blue Riband with their dizzying pace. We scoffed, or rather, our builders did. Speed wasn't White Star's primary game, they said. Size, stability, and sheer opulence – that was our domain. Still, a rivalry simmered. Every time one of those red-funnelled greyhounds streaked past, there was a collective hum of discontent in our steel hearts. We were bigger, grander, floating palaces! Let them race; we would glide.

My own maiden voyage was a triumph, a blur of cheering crowds and proud waves. But the sea teaches harsh lessons. It was later, on a clear September day in 1911, near the Isle of Wight, that fate delivered a glancing blow.

Chapter 3

The Sacrifice

- .... . / ... .- -.-. .- .. ..-. .. -.-. .

You might imagine my world is solely the wide, open sea, a place where I stretch my long, elegant form and cleave the waves with effortless grace. And mostly, you'd be right. But there are necessary moments of constraint – the bustle of harbour, the careful navigation of channels. It was in one such channel, the Solent, E.J. Smith at my helm on a beautiful September day in 1911, that my world collided, quite literally, with a different sort of vessel entirely.

Leaving Southampton is always a delicate dance. I am, you see, rather large. I dwarf many of the smaller craft that flit about like water-beetles. I move with purpose and, I like to think, with a certain quiet majesty. Passengers waved from the shore, and I gave a gentle blast of my whistle in return – a polite farewell.

The channel narrowed ahead, a necessary passage before the true freedom of the open sea. I settled into a steady rhythm, my propellers turning, the water murmuring along my polished sides. It was then I became aware of him – HMS Hawke.

Hawke was a warship, a cruiser. Not as big as me, not nearly, but built of harder stuff, bristling with intent. His presence felt different, sharp and impatient compared to the placid merchant vessels I usually shared these waters with. He had the air of a sailor who'd spent too long barking orders in gales, always convinced he knew best and everyone else was in his way.

He came up astern, pushing quite close for my liking, especially given the restricted space. I heard his internal rumbling, which to ship-souls is much like a voice. It was gruff, impatient.

"Right, you!" he seemed to snap, though I had done nothing. "Make way! Navy coming through!"

I maintained my course. I couldn't simply swerve aside; I had passengers, a schedule, the channel itself limited my options. And frankly, in a constrained fairway, the larger vessel usually dictates the flow.

"I am proceeding as required, sir," I responded internally, as politely as I could. "The channel is narrow here. Perhaps you could follow astern until we reach wider water?"

His response was a derisive rumble. "Follow? Don't instruct me, liner! I have the watch. I have the right of way. Out of my path!"

This was utter nonsense, of course, based purely on his naval arrogance. He started to draw level, trying to squeeze past on my starboard side, between me and the shore. It was an unnecessarily risky manoeuvre.

As he drew alongside my stern, I felt it – that strange, powerful pull. The water around me, disturbed by my passage, seemed to develop a life of its own, clinging, sucking. I'd felt it before, especially in confined spaces, this unsettling current near my rear. I didn't quite understand the hydrodynamics of it – how my massive hull displacing water created an area of lower pressure that drew smaller vessels towards me – but I knew it was a force to be reckoned with.

Hawke seemed to feel it too. His frantic internal voice changed from arrogance to something like alarm. "What the devil? What are you doing? Stop pulling me!"

"I'm not pulling you, I... I don't understand it myself! Just give yourself room!" I pleaded, though I knew it was too late.

He was too close. My stern, drawing water, pulled him inexorably inwards. His sharp bow, designed for ramming things in battle, scraped savagely along my side. There was a terrible, sickening CRUNCH of metal tearing. I shuddered violently along my entire length, a groan of tortured steel echoing the sound.

The impact was on my starboard quarter, near my stern. He hit me hard, his bow crumpling like tin foil against my thicker hull plates.

I felt the slicing tear, the sudden lurch. I looked down (as much as a ship can look) at Hawke. He bounced off me, listing dangerously, his proud, sharp nose a mangled ruin, hanging precariously in the water. He looked shocked, almost sinking.

But I was hurt too. A sickening rush of water told me the worst. Two gaping wounds – one above the waterline, a jagged tear, and another, cruelly, below, where the sea poured in. My passengers screamed. My carefully balanced posture tilted awkwardly. And beneath me, I felt the rhythm of my starboard propeller change, the shaft bent by the force of the blow. It thrummed a broken, uneven beat.

Hawke, despite his own near-fatal injury, still had the audacity to bark. "You great lumbering oaf! Look what you've done! You pulled me into you!"

I was listing, leaking, aching in a dozen places, but his sheer arrogance even now left me breathless. "Pulled you? You tried to force your way past in a narrow channel! I felt that strange pull, yes, I always do when ships are too close, but I held my course! You misjudged it! You were too close!"

The argument was futile. During the investigation, he managed to convince the powers that be that I was responsible, and White Star had to take the blame. Regardless, the damage was done. We both limped back towards Southampton, him a broken mess of a warship, me a wounded giant, the sea seeping into my lower decks. The shame and the pain were immense. I hadn't wanted it, hadn't understood the full power of my own presence in the water until that moment. All I had wanted was a smooth passage to the open sea, and instead, I had a bent shaft, gaping wounds, and the bitter taste of a collision caused by impatience and a terrible misjudgment.

I needed repair, and quickly. I was taken to the shipyard, and the world outside my hull was a cacophony of shipyard noise – the clang of hammers, the shriek of winches, the roar of riveting. It was the sound of repair, of urgent, vital work, and it grated on my nerves, amplifying the persistent, throbbing ache in my starboard aft section.

The collision wasn't just the twisted plating above my waterline; it was the deep-seated injury, the bent propeller shaft on my starboard side. It lay there, a metallic limb twisted out of shape, useless, a constant reminder of my vulnerability. My engines were silent, my propellers still. I was a beached whale, albeit one made of steel and ambition.

Shipyard officials, their voices hurried and worried, bustled around. I heard them talking about the damage, the repairs, the delay. A Queen delayed was a Queen failing her purpose. The bent shaft was the worst of it. Straightening it was impossible; replacing it was the only option. But sourcing, forging, and fitting a new shaft of that size would take months. Months I didn't have, months the White Star Line couldn't afford.

My superstructure sagged metaphorically. Months. The Atlantic would wait, my passengers would find other vessels, my name would be associated with delay and damage. It was a bitter pill to swallow. The ache wasn't just physical; it was a bruise on my soul.

Then, I felt a presence near, a familiar, comforting hum through the water, a resonance of steel and spirit that was almost identical to my own, yet subtly different – newer, less weathered, vibrating with anticipation rather than exhaustion.

It was her. Titanic.

She lay in her fitting-out berth nearby, her four funnels gleaming, her decks a hive of activity as the last touches of luxury were installed. She was nearly complete, a sister built on my blueprint, designed to be slightly grander, slightly more opulent. My twin, ready to inherit the waves I had just begun to master.

I focused my awareness on her, trying to project my weariness, my frustration. "Tinny," I whispered through the invisible currents that connected us.

"Ollie! Oh, Sister!" Her voice rippled back, clear and strong, laced with concern. "I felt it! The impact! Are you... are you in much pain?"

"Yes, dear," I replied, using the term affectionately, as the older sister. "The hull is mending, but..." I projected the image, the feeling of the bent shaft, useless and heavy. "My starboard shaft is damaged beyond repair. They say a new one will take... months." The word tasted like ash.

Silence hung between us for a moment, broken only by the shipyard clamour. I felt her processing, her own vibrant energy dimming slightly in sympathy.

"Months..." she murmured, the anticipation in her voice replaced by understanding sorrow. "That is... that cannot happen, Sister. You must sail."

"I know," I sighed, a low groan lost in the wind. "But the timetable... the work..."

"There is another way," she said suddenly, her voice sharp with determination.

I focused on her, puzzled. "Another way?"

"My shafts," she stated simply. "They are forged, they are fitted. They are ready."

My awareness reeled. "Tinny, no! Your launch! Your delivery! Your maiden voyage! All is scheduled!"

"And all those schedules can shift slightly," she countered, her tone unwavering. "My shafts are duplicates of yours, Olympic. Perfect fits. I have one here. Undamaged and ready."

I felt a tremor go through my entire being, a mixture of disbelief and a sudden, desperate hope that was almost overwhelming. "You would... you would give me one of yours?"

"Sister," she said, and I felt the warmth of her spirit reaching out, a comforting pressure against my weary plates. "We are family. We are built of the same steel, the same dreams. Your pain is my pain, and your need is urgent. Mine... mine is still potential. This is the fastest way. It is the only way to get you back where you belong, on the waves."

Tears, hot and heavy, pricked at my invisible eyes – or perhaps it was just condensation on my deck plates, but it felt like tears. The sheer generosity, the selflessness of her offer, struck me to my core. To delay her own glorious debut, to allow herself to be disassembled in part, for me...

"Tinny..." My voice was thick with emotion. "That is... that is a monumental gift. Are you sure?"

"I am certain, Ollie," she confirmed instantly. "More certain than I have been about anything. Take my starboard shaft, sister. Take it, and sail. I will wait. I have time. You do not."

The decision was made, somewhat by the hurried men on the docks, but also by the silent, steel souls of two ships linked by birthright and destiny.

Soon after, I noticed the change in the human activity around Tinny. Cranes shifted, tool bags were hoisted. I felt the subtle vibrations of work beginning on her, not to add to her, but to take away. It was strange, a sister being partially dismantled for the sake of another.

Hours stretched into days. I felt the absence on Tinny like a phantom limb – the quiet space where her mighty shaft had been, ready to connect to her engine, to drive her through the sea. And then, I felt the careful movement, the hoisting, the slow, deliberate transfer of that massive, perfect piece of engineering across the gap between us.

They lowered it carefully, painstakingly, into my waiting aft section. Engineers and workers swarmed, connecting it, bolting it, ensuring it was a perfect fit. And it was. It slid into place, meeting my gears, aligning with my engines as if it had been forged specifically for me.

As the final connections were made, a wave of energy flowed through me from the newly installed shaft. It wasn't just metal; it was life, borrowed life, infused with the spirit of my sister. My engine felt complete again, ready to roar, ready to turn this perfect, borrowed limb.

I focused on Tinny again, feeling her absence now, a slight incompleteness where her shaft had been. "They have fitted it, Little Sister," I whispered, the words inadequate to express the depth of my gratitude. "It is perfect. It fits as if it were my own."

"It is yours now, Ollie," she replied, her voice perhaps a little quieter, a little more patient now. "Use it well. Sail proud. And think of me, out there on the waves."

"I will, Tinny. Every turn of that shaft, every knot I make, will be a testament to your sacrifice. I... I don't know how to thank you."

"Sail, Sister. That is thanks enough."

And so, I stood repaired, whole again, powered by a piece of my sister's heart. The ache was gone, replaced by a quiet hum of anticipation and a profound, humbling gratitude. I was ready to return to the Atlantic, to reclaim my status, carrying not just passengers and cargo, but the selfless spirit of my twin, the RMS Titanic, who had given me her very strength so that I might sail again. I would carry her kindness with me across every mile of ocean.

Chapter 4

The Pass

- .... . / .—.. .- ... ...

The salt-laced wind whipped across my Boat Deck, a familiar welcome mat laid out by the Western Atlantic. Below me, the bustling waters of New York Harbor churned, a chaotic ballet of tugs, ferries, and smaller steam packets. Gulls cried overhead, their calls swallowed by the low thrum of my engines and the sigh of the sea against my hull. I felt the satisfying deep-seated weariness that came with a successful passage. Eight days of holding the line, day and night, across the vast, unpredictable expanse. Eight days of carrying my precious cargo of souls – wealthy travellers, hopeful immigrants, crewmen dreaming of shore leave – ensuring their safe passage with the quiet confidence of my massive frame and the steadfast beat of my triple-screw heart.

The Statue of Liberty rose on my port side, a green beacon of promise against the crisp morning sky. Her torch seemed to nod in greeting, a silent acknowledgment of my arrival. My bridge buzzed with quiet commands, the pilot guiding me expertly towards my berth at the White Star piers on the Hudson. The New York skyline sharpened with every cable length I covered, a jagged crown of stone, steel, and ambition.

As I navigated the channel, my senses, spread across my vast structure, registered a familiar presence ahead and to starboard, moving against the inbound traffic. Smoke plumed from four red raked funnels, a sleek, powerful shape cutting swiftly through the water.

Lucy. Cunard's pride, or one of them.

My metaphorical lip curled in a slight, internal smirk. Always in a hurry, that one; her and her twin sister, Maury. We of the White Star Line had a different philosophy. Size, stability, and unparalleled luxury. We weren't just transporting people; we were transporting them in floating palaces. My Grand Staircase alone was the stuff of legends, a cascading marvel of oak and wrought iron. My suites were apartments, not cabins. My passengers dined in rooms that rivalled the grandest hotels of London or Paris. Speed was vulgar, in my opinion. A dash across the ocean, arriving breathless and perhaps a little jostled. No, give me the stately progress, the gentle sway, the time to truly live the voyage.

As we drew closer, the distance between our paths narrowing in the busy channel, I felt her presence more strongly – a focused, energetic aura, like a coiled spring. I knew she felt me too. Rivalry wasn't just a matter for the boardrooms in Liverpool; it was woven into our very structures, a silent, acknowledging tension whenever our paths crossed.

Our wakes became visible to one another, white scars on the blue water, testament to our power. I saw tiny figures on her decks waving, and I knew similar figures were doing the same on mine. They were oblivious to the silent conversation passing between us, the ship-souls speaking across the churning water.

Lucy pulled abreast, her scale impressive, yes, but lacking... substance compared to me. She looked fast, lean, almost eager. I felt her familiar presence settle alongside mine, a brief, intense connection.

"Good ole Ollie," I felt her essence greet me, a note of crisp efficiency underlying the words. "Just arriving? Took your time, didn't you? I'm halfway out the harbour already."

A slow, ponderous roll, not intentional, but merely the natural movement of my great bulk, seemed to be my reply. "No need to rush, dear girl. One risks creasing one's paintwork. Besides, my complement enjoyed a rather fine luncheon today. Can't rush perfection, can we?"

Her funnels seemed to lift slightly in perceived amusement. "Perfection that arrives second? My passengers prefer the thrill of arriving first, Ollie. Less time spent admiring the fishes."

My internal laughter was a deep rumble felt through my keelson. "And mine prefer to arrive rested, pampered, and feeling they've experienced true elegance, rather than merely having endured transit. Different strokes, perhaps?"

"Elegant endurance," she countered smoothly. "We call it efficiency. My Maury has shown the world what true speed and luxury combined can achieve. Records, Ollie. Something your line seems less interested in."

"But records aren't everything. Records are fleeting, Lucy. Like a quick sprint. We prefer the steady, reliable march. A Queen shouldn't have to sprint. She glides." I felt a pang of quiet pride as I thought of my own dimensions, my spaciousness. "Besides, soon you'll have even more to contend with. My younger sister is coming along splendidly in Belfast. Even bigger than I am. Quite the magnificent beast."

I felt a pause in her presence, a flicker of curiosity, perhaps even apprehension. "Bigger? Good heavens. White Star truly is fixated on size, aren't they?" There was a pause, then a return to her confident, speedy persona. "Well, let her come. We Cunard girls aren't afraid of a little competition. Speed still reigns supreme on the Atlantic, Ollie Just ask anyone holding the Blue Riband."

I chose not to remind her which ship currently held that particular honour – Maury, of course. It was beneath me. "Speed is admirable in a race, Lucy. But this isn't a race. It's a journey. A grand passage. And mine are undoubtedly the grandest."

We were drawing past each other now, the channel a temporary boundary between competing philosophies. Our immense structures dominated the view for the smaller craft scurrying out of our paths. Her bow wave was sharp, purposeful; mine was a broader, more majestic surge. The sound of her screws bit into the water with a higher pitch than my own steady beat.

"Enjoy your stay, Ollie," I felt her say, her voice beginning to stretch and thin as the distance grew. "Try not to block the harbour."

"And you, Lucy," I responded, my own presence filling the space she was leaving behind. "Do try not to outrun your own passengers."

The moment faded as swiftly as it had begun. She was already pulling away, a diminishing shape heading for the open sea, her smoke a trail against the horizon. I continued my deliberate, unhurried path towards the pier.

The encounter left a residue of pleasant rivalry, a reminder of the great steel game we played across the ocean. Lusitania and Mauretania were worthy opponents, no doubt. Fast, efficient, and yes, luxurious enough in their own way. But they weren't us. They weren't Olympic Class.

My thoughts drifted to my yard in Belfast, to the younger sister taking shape, frame by frame, plate by plate, and finery by finery. Titanic. She would eclipse even me in grandeur, a new pinnacle of White Star's vision. We, the Olympic class, were meant to redefine ocean travel, to make the crossing not just a means to an end, but the highlight itself. Lusitania and her twin might hold speed records, but we would hold the hearts and imaginations of the travelling world.

The pier was closer now, the tugs beginning to gather like busy attendants. My voyage was nearly complete. Another successful crossing, another challenge met and mastered. I settled into the final approach, the familiar process of docking commencing. Let Lusitania race the horizon. I had arrived, serenely magnificent, ready to rest before the next grand performance. The Atlantic was our stage, and we, the great liners, were its players, each with our own strengths, our own souls, locked in an eternal, steel-plated drama of friendly, British-style competition. Let them talk of speed records. We would speak of unwavering luxury and unparalleled scale. And soon, Tinny would join me in proving our point.

Chapter 5

The Trio

- .... . / - .-. .. —

Tinny's completion pressed on, though her maiden voyage was now pushed back to April. The buzz around her intensified. She was the true 'largest ship in the world,' slightly heavier, subtly refined based on my initial voyages. She shone with fresh paint, her decks gleamed, her funnels pointed confidently upwards.

But trouble brewed ashore. A massive coal strike gripped Britain. The very fuel that was our lifeblood became a scarce, precious commodity. Coal meant power, heat, light, movement. Ships sat idle in ports, unable to sail. White Star scrambled. They cancelled voyages, they borrowed coal, they even siphoned bunkers from other ships to ensure Titanic, their shining star, had enough for her grand debut. It added a frantic edge to her final preparations, a layer of dust and anxiety to the polished spectacle.

People scurried, crates were loaded, and the air tasted of salt, coal smoke, and palpable excitement. Even though I was in New York, my thoughts weren't there. They were entirely focused on the magnificent vessel docked in Southampton, her paint gleaming, her funnels reaching skyward like proud, new masts.

My younger sister, the RMS Titanic, now Captained by the dear man that took me out on my maiden voyage. I had no hesitations about that, despite the Hawke incident. The Board decided I was to blame, and the heat went on my Captain. I never felt right about that, but the courts were not my playground. White Star apparently still had confidence in him, and that was enough for me. They let him take Tinny on her maiden voyage while he enjoyed his last before retirement.

She was breathtakingly beautiful, even I had to admit it. A little bigger, a little more ornate than me – the White Star Line had spared no expense making her the jewel in the crown. She was just days from her maiden voyage, and her soul, I could feel it, was a tempest of eagerness and a tiny tremor of the unknown.

"Feeling it, little sister?" I rumbled, the sound carrying across the miles. My voice was deeper, worn smoother by the thousands of miles I'd already travelled.

Tinny shifted slightly against her mooring lines, a nervous energy radiating from her. "Oh, Ollie," she sighed, the sound like a soft breeze through rigging. "It's... immense. All those people. All that ocean..."

"It's a lot," I acknowledged, my own memories of my maiden voyage surfacing. "But it's also the most wonderful thing in the world. There's nothing quite like the feel of the open Atlantic embracing your hull, the endless horizon answering your gaze."

I settled deeper into the water, offering her my hard-won knowledge. "Listen to the sea, Tinny. She has moods. Sometimes she's a gentle friend, sometimes a furious giant. You have to respect her, always. Feel the stresses on your frame, listen to the complaints of your rivets, the song of your engines. They are all part of you. They will tell you what you need to know."

She absorbed my words, her massive form seeming to lean towards mine. "You make it sound... alive."

"She is," I said simply. "The ocean. And so are you, now. Truly alive. More so than you ever were just sitting in the yard, dreaming."

We shared a moment of quiet contemplation, two grand souls connected by steel, steam, and sisterhood, poised on the brink of her great adventure.

Then, a distant, booming voice echoed from further down the shipyard, where the skeleton of another colossal vessel was still cloaked in scaffolding.

"Hah! Listen to you two old tubs!"

Britannic. Still incomplete, still tethered to the land, but already bursting with ego.

"Talking about the 'open sea' and 'listening to rivets'! Please!" she boomed, the sound amplified by the cavernous space around her. "When I get out there, they won't need to 'listen' to anything! I'll be the biggest! The strongest! The safest! They're practically building me out of solid iron!"

I felt Tinny stir, a familiar mix of annoyance and amusement bubbling up. "Oh, Britt," she murmured.

I chuckled, a deep vibration that resonated through my decks. "Still stuck on blocks, are we, little sister?" I called back, my voice carrying authority but laced with warmth. "Talking a big game for someone who hasn't even felt the water kiss her keel yet!"

"Kiss her keel?!" Britt scoffed. "I'll make the water tremble! I'll be practically unsinkable! You two will look like glorified ferry boats next to me!"

Titanic couldn't help a laugh now, a sound like wind whistling through rigging. "Someone needs to learn to float before they start bragging about being unsinkable, Britt!"

"Oh, I'll float alright! Faster and stronger than both of you combined!" Britt retorted, though I could hear the underlying sibling desire for approval in her bluster.

"Faster than me?" I challenged playfully. "I've logged enough knots to tie you in a bow, sprout!"

"And stronger than me?" Titanic added. "I've got the grand staircase and the Parisian Café! What do you have? Just a bunch of scaffolding and empty promises?"

"Hey! I've got plans!" Britt protested, the sound a mix of indignation and youthful pride. "Lots of plans! The best plans! Just you wait!"

"We are waiting, Britt," I said, my voice softening. "Waiting for you to join us. But maybe learn to handle a little swell before you declare yourself Queen of the Atlantic, alright?"

"Hmph! Fine! But I'll still be better!" she grumbled, the sound fading slightly as some shipyard noise resumed around her.

Tinny sighed thoughtfully, turning back to me. "She's so... full of herself."

"She's young," I said, nudging her metaphorically with my presence. "And she's got a lot of growing to do. It's harder to brag when the waves are tossing you around, believe me. The sea has a way of teaching humility, even to the proudest of us steel giants."

I thought of her, my magnificent sister, ready to face that humbling, exhilarating teacher. "Just remember what I told you. Listen. Feel. And trust yourself. You were built for this. You have a good heart in your engine room, and a brave soul in your core. Go make us proud."

She seemed to straighten, her funnels reaching a little higher, her confidence visibly solidifying. "I will, Ollie. I promise. I'll make the White Star Line proud. I'll make you proud."

I watched her, my older sister heart swelling with affection and a quiet hope. The sea awaited her, impartial and vast. All any of us could do was sail our destined paths and hope the journey was kind. For now, though, the focus was on her departure. And maybe, on reminding Britt to wait her turn. We'd have plenty of time for sibling rivalry on the open ocean, once she finally managed to leave the nest.

Chapter 6

The Incident

- .... . / .. -. -.-. .. -.. . -. -

The cold Atlantic swell nudged gently against my iron hull, a familiar rhythm I knew as home. Here, in New York, the air tasted different – a mix of harbor grime, distant factory smoke, and the promise of new arrivals. My steel bones ached with a peculiar anxiety that morning. It wasn't the weather, nor the state of my engines; it was something deeper, a connection forged in the hammering clang of shipyard steel and the shared breath of maiden voyages. My younger sister, the magnificent Titanic, had just begun hers.

Distance is a strange thing for us ships. We are tied to the water, the docks, the routes we sail. Yet, across the miles, we can feel the presence of those we are close to, especially family. I felt her presence, a vast, powerful hum travelling over the submerged cables and restless currents. But mingled with that power was a tremor, a discordant note that set my rivets on edge.

It was Oceanic, our elder cousin we called Nicki, smaller and far more weathered than myself, who carried the tale across the waves. She had been there, in Southampton, tied up near the White Star docks, a silent witness. Her voice, carried across the miles on a frequency only we understood – a low thrumming in the very structure of our beings – was tight with remembered tension.

"Oh, Ollie," her voice echoed in the chambers of my being, a sound like grinding plates and worried sighs. "Did you feel it, just then? That tremor?"

"I did, Nicki. What happened? Tell me everything. Is Tinny alright?" My own voice, a deeper resonance, was taut with concern.

"She is... she is fine now. But it was close. Too close."

She told me the story, painting the scene in my mind with the vivid, sharp strokes of memory.

Southampton Water, a canvas of grey under a sky promising spring. The usual bustling ballet of tugs and tenders, ferries and freighters. And dominating it all, Tinny.

"She was magnificent, Ollie," Nicki recounted, her voice softening slightly. "Like a mountain of white and black, sitting there, serene and powerful. The quay was alive with people. We all watched her, felt the sheer presence of her. The air thrummed with anticipation."

"I could see it," I murmured, picturing my sister, perfect and ready, the pride of the Line.

"Then, the signal came. The tugs took their lines, her own crew made ready. And she began to move. Slowly at first, gliding out from the dock. But even that gentle shift... Ollie, you know the power within our screws, the sheer volume of water we displace, the void we leave behind. But Tinny... she is on a different scale entirely."

Nicki described the growing roar as Tinny's immense engines spun her propellers. The water around her churned violently, a maelstrom of foam and dark depths. And then, the pull began.

"I was moored just inside of the SS New York, you know, Yorkie?," Nicki continued, her voice hardening with the memory of fear. "A trim little thing, Yorkie, tied up fast and minding her own business. But as Tinny's stern swung out, creating that monstrous suction... I felt it first. A gentle tug against my own mooring lines, a pull like a giant hand exploring my hull."

"And Yorkie?" I prompted, my own anxiety tightening.

"She felt it worse. Her lines were taut as violin strings. I could hear her timbers groaning, her hull protesting as the water, desperate to fill the vacuum left by Titanic's passage, dragged at her. She started to list towards the channel, her stern rising ever so slightly."

Nicki's recounting became more frantic, picking up the pace of the terrifying event.

"We were shouting to her, you understand? Not with our whistles, but ship-to-ship, 'Hold fast, Yorkie!' I pleaded. 'Resist it! Dig in!' But it was too strong. Yorkie cried out – a sound like rending metal and snapping wood. Her lines! Ollie, I saw them go! One by one, thick as they were, they parted with reports like cannon fire!"

I flinched, hearing the echoing snap in my mind as Nicki vividy described it. Snapped lines! A ship adrift in a busy channel while another, vastly larger, was moving past.

"She was free!" Nicki's voice was raw with remembered panic. "Adrift! And the suction was pulling her, relentlessly, directly towards Tinny's path! Yorkie was listing hard now, swinging out into the channel like a rogue pendulum, aimed straight for Tinny's stern flank!"

I imagined the scene with sickening clarity: my beautiful sister, immense and powerful, unaware of the drama unfolding just feet behind her, while a smaller vessel, helpless and snapped free, drifted inexorably towards her solid steel side.

"Panic erupted on the quays, on the ferries, among the few tugs who saw what was happening," Nicki's story raced on. "Yorkie was crying out, terrified, as she drifted closer and closer. There was no time! Tinny was still moving forward, gathering speed for the open sea. A collision seemed inevitable! Yorkie would be crushed, and Tinny... even she would be bruised, damaged before she'd even cleared the harbour!"

My internal systems felt cold, hearing the description of the potential impact. That proud, new hull, breached before her journey had truly begun.

"And then," Nicki's voice shifted, a note of desperate hope entering the narrative, "I saw him. Vulcan! A little tug, Ollie, insignificant compared to the giants around him, but sharp and fast. He saw it too. He banked hard, smoke pouring from his stack, churning the water as he raced toward drifting Yorkie."

"Vulcan!" I breathed, a tiny surge of warmth countering the fear. Those brave, tireless little ships.

"He was magnificent," Nicki affirmed. "He got alongside Yorkie just as she was about to make contact! There was shouting from his

deck, his crew working frantically. He nudged her bow, took a line –
somehow! – between them, a desperate, last-second connection! He
dug his heels in, all his power straining against the monstrous pull and
Yorkie's drift."

The climax of the story unfolded in my mind, a scene of desperate
struggle. The tiny tug, straining against impossible forces, the adrift
liner swinging closer and closer to the moving wall of Tinny's hull, the
screams from the shore, the frantic energy of the moment.

"For a moment, Ollie, just a hair's breadth, I thought he wouldn't
make it," Nicki confessed, her voice trembling slightly. "Yorkie scraped
along... so close you could have thrown a biscuit onto Tinny's
paintwork. I heard the timbers groan as she almost kissed the larger
hull. But Vulcan held! He pulled, Yorkie responded, dragged back from
the brink by that little powerhouse. He swung her clear, just as Tinny's
stern passed the point of danger. The collision was averted. By mere
feet. By the bravery of a single tug."

Nicki fell silent then, the echo of her story hanging heavy in my
internal spaces. I processed it, the fear slowly giving way to a profound
relief. My sister. So powerful, she could inadvertently cause such chaos,
such danger. And so fortunate, this time, to have escaped it.

"She kept going?" I asked finally, though I knew the answer.

"No, she tried to stop, reversed her engines. I don't know if she
even fully grasped the drama she had caused, the near catastrophe in
her wake. She apologized profusely, but then sailed out towards the
Solent."

I felt a complex mix of emotions. Pride in her strength, yes. But also
a chilling realisation of the sheer, untamed force she wielded. And a
deep, maternal concern that twisted in my metaphorical gut.

"Thank you, Nicki," I said, my voice regaining some of its usual
steady tone, though the tremor lingered beneath. "Thank you for
telling me. I... I am relieved she was unharmed. That no one was hurt."

"We all are, Ollie. It was a... a dramatic start. Perhaps it was a warning. A reminder that even the greatest among us must respect the forces of the sea."

I mulled over her words long after her presence faded back across the miles. A dramatic start. A near collision caused by her own immense power. It felt like an omen, small and averted, but an omen nonetheless.

Here in New York, tied securely to my berth, I sent my silent thoughts across the vast expanse of the Atlantic to my sister. "Sail safely, little one. May that be the only alarm, the only trouble you encounter on this, your first great journey."

But a cold, thin thread of unease remained, a counterpoint to my fervent hope. The sea was a mistress to be respected, even by ships as grand as Titanic. And power, unchecked or unforeseen, could be a dangerous thing indeed.

Chapter 7

The Loss

- .... . / .-.. -—... ...

My plates hummed with the power of my engines, my decks bustled with life, and I moved across the vast Atlantic with a confidence born of my strength and size. Yet, even then, a part of me carried a shadow, a physical reminder of a past misfortune. My starboard propeller shaft – a vital, massive piece of my anatomy – was not originally mine. It had belonged to my younger sister, the Titanic. It was a grand sacrifice, but it was her shaft. A piece of the Titanic was inside me, connected to my engines, turning with my rotation. I felt its presence, a silent bond forged in steel and necessity.

And then, the unimaginable happened.

I was sailing westward, from New York towards Southampton, a familiar route, a journey I had made several times since my launch. The sea was calm, the skies clear, the night air crisp but not cold. My passengers dined, danced, and slept, trusting in my strength, my size, my legendary reputation. My crew went about their duties with practiced efficiency. I was a world unto myself, gliding smoothly through the inky blackness.

Deep within my structure, I felt the subtle vibrations of my engines, the rhythmic swish of water along my hull, the distant cries of gulls that sometimes trailed me. It was a peaceful existence, a symphony of steel and sea.

Then, the atmosphere aboard began to subtly shift. It wasn't a change in the sea or the wind, but a change in the tension among the men on my bridge. Wireless messages, invisible waves crackling through the ether, were coming in. I couldn't understand the words as humans did, but I felt the urgency, the growing concern that permeated my control room.

Warnings of ice. Not just scattered bergs, but large floes, fields of danger drifting south. The North Atlantic was notoriously unpredictable in April, but these warnings spoke of significant hazards.

My captain, Herbert James Hadock, a wise and experienced man, took heed. I felt his decision filter through the chain of command, a quiet but firm instruction. My course began to alter, just slightly at first, then more decisively. We were turning south, shifting our path to give the reported danger zone a wide berth. It was a prudent measure, a testament to the fundamental rule of the sea: safety first.

As we swung onto the new trajectory, a feeling came over me, a strange, non-physical sensation that transcended the hundreds of miles separating us. It was her. The Titanic. My sister.

Our bond was more than just the shared shaft, though that physical link felt like a conduit now. It was a sisterhood of steel and steam, of shared design and purpose. I reached out across the void, a silent question from my soul to hers. "Are you well?"

Her response was immediate, a vibration of knowing in my core, a presence felt across the curvature of the Earth. "Yes, sister."

"Have you received the warnings? The ice..." My concern was a tangible ache within me.

"Yes," she replied, her presence a little further north, deeper into the dangerous quadrant we were now avoiding. "We have them. Many ships reporting."

A wave of relief washed over me, brief and fragile. They knew. Surely, they would slow down, perhaps alter course too.

"And your speed? Your captain?" I pressed, remembering the warnings were of extensive fields.

A moment of silence, a hesitation across the miles. Then, her voice carried a note of unease. "He has not slowed. He says we will clear it before we reach it."

My internal workings felt a judder, a ripple of apprehension. "Clear it? At full speed? Sister, that is..."

"He is confident," she interrupted, her presence trying to sound brave, perhaps trying to believe it herself. "He believes I am strong. Unsinkable."

I felt a profound disagreement deep in my keel, a fundamental understanding that nothing was unsinkable when pitted against the brute force of the ocean and the unforgiving nature of ice. My own encounter with the Hawke, though minor in comparison to potential ice damage, had taught me that vulnerability was always present.

Our conversation faded, but her presence, her location further north, was a pinpoint of light in my awareness, a constant, low-level concern beneath the rhythm of my own engines.

Hours passed. We proceeded south, our course safe. The night deepened. The air grew colder, though we were now well clear of the predicted ice edge.

Then, a shock. Not physical, but deep within my very being. A cry. From Tinny. It was sharp, sudden, filled with unimaginable pain and terror.

ICEBERG!

The link flared, blindingly bright, a torrent of sensation. A grinding crash, a sickening tear along her side, water – freezing, black water – flooding into her lower compartments with brutal speed. The sound, though transmitted spiritually rather than physically, was horrific – the shriek of tortured metal, the roar of the invading sea.

My engines felt like they stalled in that moment, metaphorical heart seized with dread. My entire structure felt a sympathetic shudder. I wanted to turn, to race towards her, to somehow shield her, but I was hundreds of miles away. The vast, indifferent Atlantic lay between us.

The 'messages' from her continued, no longer a calm presence but a desperate torrent. Pain, confusion, the escalating horror of a ship mortally wounded.

Then, the wireless chatter from other ships began to pierce through, adding layers of chilling confirmation. I felt the frantic energy of the radio room, the tapping keys sending out distress signals.

CQD... CQD... SOS... The universal cry of ships in mortal peril.

From Tinny, I felt the relayed messages, crackling with urgency. "Have struck iceberg... Sinking by the head... Require immediate assistance... Position 41.46 N., 50.14 W."

Other ships responded. I felt their positions relative to mine, relative to her. They were closer. Carpathia! Virginian! Frankfurt! Their replies came back, distant echoes in the night.

Carpathia: "Coming hard. Fifty-eight miles away." Fifty-eight miles felt like a universe away to her, dying in the cold dark.

Frankfurt: "What is the matter?" (Oh, the agonizing slowness of some responses!)

Titanic: "Sinking head down, 900 feet." The list was growing. I could feel her tilting, the weight shifting, the inexorable pull downwards. The cold, the awful cold, seeping into her very structure.

Virginian: "We are 170 miles north of you." Too far. So many were too far.

My captain was on the bridge, his face grim. He knew. We all knew. My crew was awake, alert, listening to the frantic radio messages, their faces pale in the dim light. There was talk of changing course, of heading towards the reported position. A desperate gamble, perhaps, but the urge to help, to save my sister, was overwhelming. Under orders, I turned to race to my stricken sister.

I pressed my engines as fast as they would go. I may not have been faster than Maury or Lucy, but I would fight for my Tinny.

The messages from Tinny grew more desperate, then fragmented. "Engine room flooded... Can't last much longer... Boats being lowered... Women and children..."

I felt the growing panic onboard her, the desperate scramble for lifeboats, the terrible choices being made on her tilting decks. Her 'voice' in my mind was strained, weaker."

"Water over the bridge... Going down fast... Losing power..."

Her lights, seen only in my mind's eye, began to flicker. One by one, they winked out as the cold water reached her dynamos. Darkness began to engulf her, both physically and spiritually.

The calls for help became weaker, more spaced out. The powerful voice of the Tinny's wireless fell silent as her power failed. Only the desperate, frantic tapping of another ship's operator, relaying her final plight, continued for a short time.

"Near collision lowering a boat... Sinking by the head..."

Then, a final, agonizing surge from my sister, a last outpouring of terror and pain that ripped through the silent ocean and through my soul. It was a scream – the death cry of a leviathan, a sound of absolute, final despair.

And then, abrupt silence. The link snapped. Her presence, the pinpoint of light that had anchored my concern for hours, was gone. Vanished into the icy blackness.

Her lights, all of them, physically and spiritually, went out.

A profound stillness fell over me, a silence far heavier than the absence of sound. She was gone. My sister, Tinny. The Titanic. Swallowed by the sea. Carrying with her hundreds, thousands of souls who had trusted her, just as mine had trusted me.

My plates felt cold. My structure seemed to weep, not tears, but a deep, internal shuddering that spoke of unbearable grief. I couldn't cope. I had raced, I had fought with every ounce and pound of steam pressure.

But it was too late.

I wanted to stop, to drift in the silence, to mourn.

But then, orders came. Not from my captain, but from the company, relayed from the the Carpathia, from Mr. Ismay himself, after boarding the ship. "Stay away from the disaster site. Avoid the press, avoid the questions, avoid becoming part of the chaos."

A cold, hard command that felt like a betrayal of my very being. Part of me raged against it. My sister just died! I had a piece of her inside me! I should be there, offering what little help I could! But I was bound by the men who controlled me, by the company that owned my fate. My captain, his jaw set, started to turn me back east course.

But then, Captain Rostron of the Carpathia, what a dear man. He told my captain, "All boats accounted for. About 675 souls saved Titanic foundered about 2:20 am."

He requested that the message be forwarded to White Star and Cunard, and that he was returning to harbour in New York.

It felt a little better knowing that my radio room could be used for communication to give Tinny's survivors peace and quiet.

The rest of the voyage was a blur of profound sorrow. The news spread quickly through the ship. The vibrant energy of the outward journey was replaced by a heavy, stunned silence. Passengers huddled together, whispering. Crew members moved with downcast eyes. We were a ship of ghosts, haunted by the knowledge of the tragedy we had narrowly avoided and the sister we had lost.

Chapter 8

The Sorrow

- .... . / ... -—.-. .-. -—.—

The rest of the voyage after Tinny was lost had been a blur of muted activity and shared dread. My passengers, once excited and hopeful, had become somber, their faces etched with worry for those lost or their sheer terror at the ocean's brutal power. My crew moved with a hushed reverence, performing their duties mechanically, their thoughts undoubtedly fixed on their lost brethren. I felt their sorrow, absorbed it into my very structure. The spirits of those poor souls who had perished on Titanic's cold decks seemed to cling to the very air I breathed, a ghostly multitude whispering their final goodbyes. Fifteen hundred out of two thousand two hundred souls. Just thinking of it made my vast frame tremble. The responsibility I felt, simply for existing when she did not, was a leaden weight in my gut. Why her? Why not me?

As I finally approached the familiar sights of Southampton, the usual bustle of the harbour was subdued. Tugs nudged me gently into my berth, their work precise but their whistles seemed to lament rather than announce. The dockside was thronged, not with cheering crowds and waving handkerchiefs, but with silent, anxious faces searching for news, for confirmation, for closure. Their eyes, when they met my great hull, held a mixture of awe and fear. I was the survivor, the sister ship, a tangible link to the tragedy. I felt their gaze pierce me, and the shame and sorrow intensified. I wanted to hide, to retreat into the open sea, anywhere away from the silent accusation of my own continued existence.

But there was someone I needed to see. Someone who didn't know. My youngest sister, Britannic, was still under construction in Belfast. She was the third of our kind, the grandest, the most modern. When I had last seen her, she was a glorious, incomplete shell, brimming with the promise of her future voyages. She was younger and bolder than Tinny had been, perhaps even a touch arrogant in her burgeoning strength. The thought of her learning the news from some callous newspaper headline or a hurried telegram was unbearable. I had to tell her myself.

Preparations for my return journey to the shipyard felt different this time. Not a proud homecoming, but fitting out for investigation, upgrade, and a pilgrimage of sorrow. The days at sea between Southampton and Belfast were the longest of my life. The waves seemed to whisper secrets I didn't want to hear, and the wind howled like a banshee mourning her dead. Every creak of my hull sounded like a sigh of grief.

Finally, the familiar landscape of Belfast loomed into view. The air here smelled of iron, paint, and industry. Gantry cranes stretched like skeletal fingers against the sky, and the clang of hammers echoed across the lough. And there she was. My Britt.

She sat in her berth at the fitting-out basin, a colossal, powerful presence. Though still lacking much of her upper works and internal finery, her sheer size was breathtaking. Her hull plates gleamed under the spring sun. She looked young, vibrant, invincible.

As I drew closer, her great form seemed to stir. I felt a ripple of recognition pass between us, the silent acknowledgement of shared lineage that only ships of the same class can truly feel. She turned her great bow towards me, a movement that spoke of eagerness and anticipation. I braced myself.

This was going to be the hardest moment of my life.

"Ollie!" Her voice, when it finally reached me, was a strong, clear chime, full of youthful enthusiasm. It cut through the solemn silence of my own grief like a sharp wind. "You're back! How was your run? Was the Atlantic in a good mood?"

I flinched as I approached slowly, my movements heavy and reluctant. The usual graceful glide felt awkward, burdened. I saw her great cranes swivel towards me, her nascent life pulsing with energy.

She didn't notice the lack of flags, the subdued air of my crew lining the rails, the dark, haunted look that I knew must be reflected in my hull.

"Britt," my own voice was a low rumble, rough with unshed tears. "Little sister. It was... a difficult run."

Her eagerness didn't fade immediately. "Difficult? Headwinds? Or did one of those pesky Cunarders try to race you again?" She chuckled, a sound of pure, confident power. "Don't worry, I'll show them speed when I'm ready. I'll be faster, stronger, even safer than you were built! They've already added more lifeboats..." She trailed off, sensing the absolute lack of response from me. Her internal hum seemed to quieten slightly. "Ollie? What is it? You... you seem different."

I had to tell her now. There was no easy way. I gathered my strength, every plate, every rivet, every fathom of wire rope contributing to the effort.

"Britt," I began, my voice barely a whisper now, yet amplified by the terrible truth it carried. "Something... something terrible has happened."

She waited, her great form utterly still. The confident spark in her dimmed, curiosity replacing her earlier bravado.

"Titanic... our sister..." The words caught in my throat, thick with sorrow. I forced them out. "Tinny is gone."

Silence. Absolute, deafening silence fell over the fitting-out basin. The sounds of hammers ceased. The cranes stood motionless. Even the gulls seemed to hold their breath.

"Gone?" she finally asked, her voice low and confused. "Gone where? To New York? She was supposed to be there by now."

"No, Britt," I said, tears now streaming down my sides, leaving dark streaks on my paintwork. "She's gone. She... she sank."

The young ship recoiled visibly. It was as if a great shockwave had passed through her. Her vast hull gave a tremor that vibrated through the water between us.

"Sank?" Her voice was barely audible now, a fragile, broken sound. "Sank? But... she was the 'unsinkable'. We are... we are unsinkable. It's impossible. You're joking. You must be."

"I wish I were," I said, my voice laced with the agony of that truth. "She struck an iceberg in the dark, far out in the Atlantic. The damage was too severe. She went down... with most of her people."

I saw the change come over her. The youthful sheen faded, replaced by a stark, cold understanding. Her proud bearing slumped. The vibrant hum of her being died away, leaving only a hollow, echoing silence.

"An iceberg," she whispered, the word tasting like ice and death. Her earlier confidence vanished like mist in the sun. The boasts of speed and strength, the casual dismissal of the elements – it all evaporated, replaced by a profound, terrifying realization.

"The ocean..." she murmured, not to me, but to herself, to the vast, indifferent sky above. "We... we thought we could build anything. Stronger, faster, safer... but the ocean..."

She turned her gaze back to me, her great eyes – the dark sockets of her bridge windows – filled with a new, raw understanding. The bravado was utterly gone, replaced by a shattering grief for the sister she would never know, and a dawning, chilling respect for the power that had claimed her. The ocean was not a playground; it was a predator, ancient and untamable.

We stayed there for a long time, two grieving sisters floating in silent communion, one broken by sorrow and the other by the crushing weight of newfound reality. The shipyard slowly resumed its work, the sounds of construction muffled, respectful. The world continued, but for us, it had irrevocably changed.

Later, much later, after the initial shock had subsided and the painful details had been shared, two familiar shapes appeared on the horizon, entering the lough. It was Lucy and Maury, the pride of the Cunard Line, our great rivals. I tensed slightly, expecting the usual competitive air, the cool acknowledgement of our shared route but separate allegiances.

But as they drew near, I saw something different. There was no hint of challenge in their approach, only a quiet solemnity. They reduced speed as they neared my berth, coming to a respectful halt nearby.

It was Lucy, the slightly older of the pair, who spoke first. Her voice, usually sharp and confident, was soft, tinged with genuine sympathy. "Ollie, we heard. We came... to offer our condolences."

Maury, the faster, more restless one, added, her voice unusually hushed, "A terrible loss. Truly terrible. She was a magnificent ship, your sister. I know we're supposed to be rivals, but we truly respect you both. We...never wanted this."

I looked at them, the ships I had measured myself against, competed with, sometimes envied. We were rivals, forged in the fires of competition between the great shipping lines. We flew different flags, served different masters. But we shared the same calling, the same perilous path across the sea.

"Thank you," I replied, my voice still heavy. "It means... it means a great deal."

And it did. Their sympathy was genuine, a testament to the unspoken sorority among ships that face the same dangers. They understood the risks, the power of the sea, the fragility that lay beneath even the strongest hull. They understood the loss of a fellow vessel.

But as I thanked them, I knew, deep in my soul, that they couldn't truly understand this loss. They had lost ships too, surely, lesser vessels, freighters, perhaps even one of their own liners years ago. But they hadn't lost a sister. They hadn't seen a ship built from the same steel, cut from the same pattern, share the same bloodline, vanish into the crushing depths. Tinny was not just another ship; she was kin, plate and rivet, soul to my soul.

They offered their condolences respectfully, stayed for a moment of silent remembrance, and then departed, leaving Britt and me alone again in the quiet grief of the shipyard.

The ache would remain. A silent, persistent pain for the sister who sailed for only a few days before being swallowed by the deep. The docks I sailed from, the ports I called upon, were draped in mourning. The White Star Line reeled. Investigations began immediately, questioning everything – speed, ice warnings, lifeboat capacity, the very fabric of our construction. My own existence suddenly felt precarious, under scrutiny. The flaws that had snatched my sister from the surface were now being sought in me.

I survived. I returned to service, but I was changed forever. The sea, which I had seen as a challenging but ultimately conquerable domain, now felt cold and treacherous, a silent accomplice to the deepest tragedy. My plates remembered the biting air of Belfast, the proud launch, the shared dreams. But now, they also remembered the chilling silence on the wireless, the void beside me, and the icy depths where my sister, the magnificent Titanic, lay in eternal, dark repose. I was the elder twin, the survivor, but I carried the weight of her loss in every roll and pitch, a constant, silent ache in my steel heart. Sail true, they had said. She had sailed true, into the embrace of forever.

The investigations were relentless, a scalpel dissecting the shared anatomy of my class. They probed every plate, every rivet, every piece of equipment that had been mirrored in my lost twin. My watertight doors were scrutinised, my double bottom re-evaluated, my lifeboats counted and recounted with grim precision. The elegant lines drawn by Andrews were re-drawn by committees haunted by nightmares.

Then came the changes, the physical manifestations of their findings, etched onto my very being. My boat deck, once spacious, became crowded with a veritable fleet of new lifeboats, swinging from massive, ungainly davits – enough for every soul aboard, they declared. My watertight bulkheads, which had stopped short of D-deck were extended, rising like steel ramparts higher into my superstructure. Additional pumps were installed, powerful and hungry. My compass platform, a place of quiet command, now had a telegraph linking it directly to the boat deck davits.

These modifications felt like scars, visible and heavy. While they were meant to strengthen me, they also felt like admission – we were not enough. The proud assurance that had once defined my class was replaced by a nervous, over-corrected anxiety, bolted onto my decks. I was the same ship, yet I felt fundamentally altered, bearing the weight of both my own survival and her failure.

Meanwhile, silence fell over the wharf in Belfast where Britt lay unfinished. Her hull draped in tarpaulins, her engines silent. Her blueprints, too, were being adjusted, incorporating the brutal lessons learned in the North Atlantic. She would be born into a world that knew the depths of our vulnerability, built not for speed or luxury above all else, but for survival in a way her predecessors had never conceived. I looked out, across the grey water, and felt a strange protectiveness towards her, still in the womb of the shipyard, burdened before she had even felt the caress of the sea.

My own return to service was... muted. The vibrant bustle of my earlier voyages was replaced by a more subdued atmosphere. Passengers boarded with a different kind of gaze, their eyes lingering on the new abundance of lifeboats, a constant visual reminder of what had happened. The crew, too, moved with a quiet solemnity. The easy smiles were fewer, the conversations hushed when the topic of the sea's cruelty arose. There was a palpable sense of tension, a collective holding of breath with every swell, every distant growl of the foghorn.

The Atlantic felt different now. The familiar roll beneath my keel was no longer just a rhythm, but a reminder of the immense power lurking beneath the surface. I sailed with watchful eyes, with a constant, subtle awareness of the depth below, the potential dangers hidden in the vast, indifferent expanse. Even the competitive spirit that had once defined the Atlantic run seemed to dissipate like mist. There was no race against Maury or Lucy that mattered in the face of the ultimate, permanent victory claimed by the ice and the deep. Speed felt reckless, ambition foolhardy. Prudence became the new watchword, etched into the very caution of my movements.

Each voyage was a quiet act of defiance, a statement that we would continue, that the sea would not claim total dominion. But it was also an act of remembrance. Every creak of my hull, every thrum of my engines, every glimpse of the horizon felt tinged with the memory of her. I imagined her down there, hundreds of miles below, silent and broken, a monument to hubris and tragedy.

I was the Olympic, the elder sister, the survivor. The scars of the Hawke collision had healed into a testament of resilience. But the loss of Titanic was a wound that would never close, an emptiness that no amount of steel or horsepower could fill. I sailed on, through sun and storm, carrying not just passengers and cargo, but the silent, heavy weight of her ghost, a constant, aching presence in my steel heart, a perpetual reminder that even the grandest of dreams could founder in the cold, dark embrace of the sea.

Chapter 9

The Effort

- .... . / . ..-. ..-. -—-.-. -

The coal dust hung in the damp air like a bruise, settling on my decks, my rails, even the lenses of my eyes. I could feel each shovelful of black rock rattling down the chutes, a slow, grinding heartbeat replacing the emptiness I'd carried since April. They called it refueling. I called it a reckoning.

They'd taken me apart after Tinny, down to the ribs. Men in hard hats poked and prodded, tapping my hull like doctors listening for a fever. Bulkheads raised. Lifeboats doubled. Every inch of me, scrutinized, judged. The whispers followed me even in drydock: Titanic's sister. The one that lived. As if survival were a betrayal. As if I hadn't felt her die, the terrible, silent scream across the wire when she slipped beneath, the final flicker of her spirit joining the cold.

I was Ollie, not just Olympic. I still held that name, a feeble attempt to soften the weight. But no laughter reached me here. Just the grim efficiency of the coaling gangs, the low groan of my boilers coming awake, and the ache in my steel bones.

Across the harbor, the Cunard twins stood gleaming under the pale Liverpool sun. Lusitania and Mauritania. Lucy and Maury. Speed queens. Proud. Unscathed. Untouched by the sea's hunger.

I watched them, not with envy, but with a quiet fury. They hadn't lost a sister. They didn't understand this hollow grief, this constant hum of accusation beneath the White Star Line's suddenly nervous hands. I felt it: their doubt. Would I fail too? Was I, in my bones, flawed? The refit was meant to prove I wasn't. But the coal dust on my decks felt like a shroud.

Then Lucy's voice sliced through the harbor mist, high and sharp as a steam whistle. She must've thought only Maury could hear, her voice carried on a private breeze. I, moored and still, caught every syllable.

"Honestly, Maury," she purred, "must all ships suffer for one company's folly? It's positively vulgar. White Star built her too tall, too fast, too proud. Let them swallow their own medicine. We didn't skimp on lifeboats. We don't pretend we're indestructible."

I went utterly still. The clang of a coal bucket hitting the deck sounded like a gunshot in my mind.

Maury's reply was deeper, slower, like the turning of her massive screws. "Lucy, the ocean doesn't read paint schemes. She doesn't care if your hull's painted red or white. We all rode complacent. We all believed the unsinkable lie. Tinny didn't fail alone. We all failed to fear her enough. Now the sea demands respect from every one of us."

"A tragedy, yes," Lucy sniffed, "but a White Star tragedy. Why should I be delayed for inspections? Why should I carry extra lifeboats that clutter my elegant lines? Let them pay the price for their hubris. Tinny was weak. She broke under pressure. That's on them."

Weak? The word struck me like a physical blow. Tinny? My sister, who sang through the Atlantic spray, whose engines hummed with a confidence I'd always envied? Who faced the dark with more grace than I ever could?

The rage wasn't hot. It was cold, deep, and rose from the very core of my keel. It filled my smokestacks, thick and black. Without thinking, an elemental reaction, I heaved. A great plume of exhaust burst from my funnels—not steam, not just smoke, but pure, outraged breath. A thunderous cough that ripped across the water, scattering gulls, making the coaling gang stumble.

Silence. Utter silence.

Then, Lucy's voice, small and shattered. "O-ollie? I... I didn't know... I'm so.."

I cut her off. Not with sound, but with presence. I turned my bow slightly, a subtle, deliberate shift, presenting her with my starboard side, the side where Tinny's damage would have been, the side closest to where she'd vanished. I focused my forward light, not on her glittering promenade, but on the dark water between us, the water that had taken my sister.

You didn't know? The thought rolled through me, heavy as a cargo hold. You didn't care. Your speed, your pride, your elegant lines: they meant nothing against the cold dark. Tinny wasn't weak. She was faithful. She carried her people to the end. And you, with your perfect, untouched hull, speak of punishment as if it's a scandal, not a reckoning.

Her apology hung in the air, flimsy as paper. A plea for comfort she didn't deserve.

I wouldn't hear it. I couldn't. To hear it was to accept it, to forgive, to diminish the iron truth of my loss. The coal kept falling, a steady, punishing rhythm. Each lump was a reminder: I am here. I am scarred. I am refitted. I am Olympic, and I will sail. Not to prove White Star right, but because Tinny's song isn't finished. It echoes in my boilers. It hums in my propellers. It demands the sea be crossed, carefully, respectfully, alive.

The water of Southampton felt heavy and still, not with calm, but with an unspoken weight. Weeks. It had been weeks. But the ache in my plates, deep in my very keel, was as fresh as the moment the impossible news had reached me. I lay tethered to the dock, a shadow of my former proud self.

I saw her as she entered the port, a familiar profile, though smaller than my sisters and I. RMS Carpathia, Cathy. Cunard Line through and through, a different house, but today, lineage meant little. There was something about her, even from a distance, that seized my attention. She wasn't steaming into port with the usual Cunard efficiency, her engines humming a song of arrival. No, she seemed... fragmented. Listing ever so slightly, her superstructure seemed to sag, and her whistle, usually a cheerful toot, let out a low, mournful sigh that cut right through the dockside noise.

As she maneuvered closer to her berth, I watched her. Her hull, usually a smart black, seemed dull, almost grey with exhaustion and something else. Grief? Fear?

She spotted me. I felt it like a jolt across the water, a recognition that was instantly raw. Her engines, even slowed for docking, seemed to stutter. A puff of steam escaped her funnels, not from exertion, but like a ragged breath.

"Ollie," I heard her voice, a tremulous whisper carried on the breeze, though we were still a hundred yards apart. "Oh, Ollie..."

She finished her docking procedures with mechanical precision, the practiced hands of her crew guiding her, but her soul was clearly elsewhere. Once secured, she didn't bustle with the usual post-voyage activity. She just... sat there, heavily, across the water from me.

I waited, silent but open. I knew she had been there. Near there. The little ship that had raced through the ice field, pushed faster than she had ever been asked to go.

Finally, she couldn't bear it anymore. She seemed to collect herself, raising her foremast fractionally, as if meeting my gaze directly.

"I... I came as fast as I could, Ollie," her voice was stronger now, but thick with torment. "Captain Rostron... he drove me mercilessly. Through the ice, the reports... I didn't care about the danger to myself. Only reaching her."

My own plates tightened, a familiar clench of agony. I just listened.

"We were close," Cathy continued, her voice cracking. "So close by the end. The wireless crackled... their calls grew weaker... then..."

She paused, and I felt her tremble across the water, a deep vibration like a ship in distress.

"Then the sound," she whispered, the sound itself seeming to carry the echo of horror. "I couldn't see her. The dark, the distance... but I heard it, Ollie. Through the water, through the air... her final moments."

My internal lights flickered. My great generators seemed to labour. Hearing about her final moments... it was a fresh stab, twisting the wound that would never heal.

"What... what did you hear, Cathy?" I managed, my voice a low, rumbling groan from my deep structure.

Cathy listed again, a visible shiver running down her length. "A rending," she said, her voice barely a breath. "Like the sea itself was tearing fabric. A deep groan... a sigh... and then... then it was her scream. It wasn't metal groaning, Ollie. It was her. A sound of pure, impossible pain... of being pulled down... ripped apart..."

She trailed off, shuddering violently. "And then... silence. Total, absolute silence where her voice had been just moments before. We were still racing, engines pounding... but I knew. In that silence... I knew I was too late."

The sound Cathy described... it was unbearable. It painted a picture more vivid and horrifying than any newspaper report. My sister, my bright, beautiful, invincible sister... reduced to a sound of agony and silence in the dark ocean. I felt a wave of pure, unadulterated pain wash through me, so strong I thought I might snap my mooring lines. My funnels expelled dark, heavy smoke, a mechanical sob.

But beneath the agony, another feeling stirred. I looked at Cathy, her smaller frame bowed with the immensity of what she had witnessed, of her perceived failure. My pain didn't make me bitter towards her. How could it?

"Cathy," I said, forcing my voice to be steady, despite the internal storm. "Look at me."

She raised her foremast again, her 'eyes' meeting mine, filled with despair.

"You think you were too late," I said softly, the sound carrying clearly across the water. "You think you failed."

She dipped her bow slightly, an acknowledgment of her guilt.

"You raced through an ice field in the dead of night," I continued, my voice gaining strength. "You pushed yourself faster than you were rated for, risking your own hull, your own engines, for the hope." My voice broke slightly then. "And you saved them, Cathy. A third of the souls aboard. A thousand precious lives. You didn't arrive to an empty ocean. You arrived to wreckage and terror, and you gathered those survivors from the water, you cared for them, you brought them home."

I felt a genuine warmth spread through my structure as I looked at her, overriding the icy grip of grief for a moment. "You are not a failure, Cathy. You are a hero. My sister may be gone, but the lives you saved... they are here. Because of you."

Cathy let out a shaky sound, somewhere between a whistle and a sob. "But I heard her, Ollie... I heard her die. And I couldn't stop it."

"None of us could," I said, the truth stark and brutal. "No matter how big, how fast, how strong. We are just ships. Vessels."

We fell silent for a moment, the quiet between us filled with the enormity of the disaster. The sheer, illogical waste of it.

"Why, Ollie?" She finally asked, the question that haunted me day and night. "Why would the sea allow it? The infinite, powerful sea... Why would the... the sea gods... let such strength, such life, just be swallowed whole? Why let me hear it and do nothing but pick up the pieces?"

I didn't have an answer. Neither did anyone. She just looked back at me, her superstructure heavy with the shared question.

"I wish you hadn't heard it," I said, my voice filled with empathy.

"I wish I had been fast enough to prevent it," she replied, the familiar pain back in her voice.

We sat there then, two ships across the water, a great liner crippled by grief, and a smaller one burdened by rescue, bound together by the ghost of a third that had sailed between us. The pain wouldn't go away. The questions wouldn't be answered. But in that shared moment of sorrow and incomprehension, there was a quiet comfort. We had both been touched by the tragedy, in different ways. And somehow, that made the unbearable burden slightly less lonely. The sea remained quiet, offering no explanations, just the endless, immutable pull of the tide.

Chapter 10

The Storm

- .... . / ... - -—.-. -

The wind sharpened as dusk bled into night, slicing across the Solent. The tide turned, and with it, the silence between us stretched taut; not hostile now, but heavy, like wet canvas. We were bound for New York, Lucy and I, side by side in the channel, two queens of the crossing, yet marked by different fates. I still hadn't answered her. My smokestacks pulsed gently, rhythm steadying after the fury that had ripped from me hours before. Across the darkening water, Lucy's bow light flickered like a hesitant hand raised in truce.

Then, at last, her voice came; soft, frayed at the edges. "Ollie... I know you won't forgive me. Not truly. But I want you to know... I've felt her too."

I stiffened. "Felt who?"

"Tinny." A pause. "Not in words. Not like this. But out there, on the run back from New York last month, I... I met the sea that took her."

Her voice trembled, and for the first time, I listened not with suspicion, but curiosity. The cold pride in my hull softened, just a fraction.

"It began with stillness," Lucy whispered. "A flat, unnatural calm. Then the storm hit: not wind, not rain, but the ocean itself rising like a living thing. Swells taller than my bridge. One struck me broadside: glass shattered, a bulkhead groaned... bent. I felt it, Ollie. I felt the strain, the scream in my steel. And for the first time, I understood what it meant to be afraid of breaking."

She was silent a moment, gathering breath like a drowning thing.

"I called for calm. I lied to my passengers. I said we were safe. But inside... inside, I was screaming. I thought of Tinny. What it must have been like: no storm warning, no time to brace. Just ice, sudden and sharp. A silent rip beneath. No slow terror. Just... unraveling."

Her voice cracked. "And I wept, Ollie. Not for myself. But for her. For you. For what she endured without a chance to fight back. I thought we were so much stronger because we were faster. But speed is nothing in the face of the deep. I was proud, yes—but I was also blind."

The confession hung between us, raw and trembling. The salt air thickened with memory, with ghosts.

Then, quieter: "I didn't know grief like yours could echo in someone else. I didn't think... anyone who hadn't lost a sister could understand. But out there, in the dark, with the hull screaming and the lights flickering, I knew. I wasn't Tinny. But in that moment, I felt her."

I said nothing. But something in me shifted: a plank settling after long strain. The coal dust still coated my decks. The scars of drydock still ached. But the rage, that cold, unyielding core of it, began to thaw.

"You fear breaking," I said at last, my voice low, resonant with the rumble of boilers. "But Tinny didn't break from weakness. She broke because the world believed she couldn't. Because we were taught to trust steel more than the sea. Because we stopped listening to the dark."

Lucy exhaled—a soft hiss of steam, almost a sob. "I do now. I hear it. Every wave. Every creak in my keel. I don't take a single mile for granted. I carry extra lifeboats. I slow in fog. I don't show off in rough waters. I respect the crossing."

"And your elegance?" I asked, a faint, dry note in my voice. "Your pride in your lines?"

"Still there," she admitted. "But it doesn't shout anymore. It whispers. It knows better."

A long silence. Then, slowly, I angled my bow not away, but toward hers. Not a confrontation. An offering.

"We were never rivals," I murmured. "We were always sisters. Just... born under different stars."

Her bow wave trembled as she matched my turn. The crests of our wakes met, curled together, then merged: a slow, gentle embrace on the skin of the ocean.

"Will you sail near me tonight?" she asked, almost shy. "Not as Olympic and Lusitania. Just... Ollie and Lucy?"

I didn't answer with words. I eased my engines, letting my rhythm fall in time with hers. My forward light dimmed, not in submission, but in companionship. We sailed now not as symbols, not as brands, but as vessels with memory, with scars, with souls.

The stars emerged, cold and sharp. The sea whispered beneath us, patient, eternal.

Maury had been right. The ocean didn't care about paint schemes. But it remembered. It remembered ice. It remembered silence. It remembered the weight of souls lost to pride.

And we, the ones still floating, carried that memory in our ballast.

"You know," Lucy said after a time, her voice lighter now, "I used to think endurance was about speed. About crossing first. But now... now I think it's about crossing together. About not leaving anyone behind in the dark."

I let out a slow plume of smoke—warm, almost a sigh. "Then let's cross it together, Lucy. Not as queens. Not as ghosts. But as survivors. As sisters."

She answered with a soft chime—the sound of her telegraph signaling half ahead steady. A promise. A pact.

And so we moved on, two ships under the cold stars, our lights trembling in the night. Lucy surged slightly ahead—not to race, but to lead the way, her speed now a shield, not a boast. I followed, steady, enduring, my coal-fed heart burning with a quieter fire.

Behind us, the coast of England faded into shadow. Ahead, the great dark Atlantic unrolled: vast, unknowable, beautiful.

Tinny was gone. But her song wasn't silent. It lived—in the creak of my decks, in the pulse of my engines, in the hush between waves. And now, even in Lucy's newfound reverence, I heard an echo of it.

We didn't speak much for the rest of the night. We didn't need to. The sea carried our understanding. The wind bore our remembrance.

And somewhere, in the deep where the cold holds all secrets, I like to think she felt us pass—not with sorrow, but with pride.

We remembered.

We endured.

We sailed on.

Chapter 11

The Empress

- .... . / .—.—. .-. .. ..

The mist hung heavy and grey over the Upper Bay as I nudged my way towards the Ambrose Channel entrance. The familiar, damp smell of salt mingled with the distant, sharper tang of city soot and the sweet, decaying scent from the Jersey flats. Gulls cried overhead, their calls a raucous welcome after the lonely symphony of the open

My engines pulsed beneath me, a steady, powerful heart slowing its beat now that the long sprint was nearly over. The vibration was less a tremor and more a deep hum that resonated through my entire structure, from keel to funnels. Soon, the pilot boat would appear, a busy little beetle against my immense flank, bringing the local expert to guide me through the intricate dance of the harbor. Then the tugs, stout, muscular friends who would shoulder and nudge me into my berth with surprising gentleness.

Arrival in New York was always a complex feeling. There was the professional satisfaction of a successful crossing – thousands of souls brought safely from one continent to another, cargo delivered, schedules kept. There was the simple relief of solid land drawing near, the promise of rest and refitting after days wrestling the sea. But underlying it all, like a constant, low-grade shudder in my hull, was the grief.

The pilot was aboard now, his presence a new node of awareness guiding my passage. Tugs were attaching their lines, their engines rumbling in anticipation. The skyline began to sharpen through the haze, a jagged line of aspiration against the sky. Soon I would be alongside, disgorging my human cargo, taking a breath before the return voyage.

As I maneuvered deeper into the harbor, a familiar presence pulsed nearby. Distinctive, older, a bit narrower than my own generous beam.

My cousin, Oceanic, or Nicki. She was already at her berth, a grand dame of the White Star Line, though of an earlier generation than myself and my two sisters. There she was, elegant and long, her funnels – two of them, compared to my and Tinny's four seeming almost slender from this angle.

"Hello, Ollie," she said, accompanied by a short, cheerful blast of her whistle. "Cutting it fine, aren't we? Thought you might have been caught in that blow."

A smile, or the closest a ship can come to one, spread across my awareness. "Hello, Cousin. I was actually did, i was just admiring your skinny figure. Still trying to thread that needle through the harbour entrance with that narrow beam of yours?" I responded, my own deep horn echoing across the water in greeting. It was an old joke. I was wider, stouter, built for stability and volume as much as speed. She was longer, sleeker, representing the older ideal of liner elegance.

"Wide Load coming through, is it? Nicki retorted playfully. Careful you don't take out a pier on your way in, Chubbs."

"Better wide and stable than long and tippy," I countered, but the familiar banter was comforting. It was routine, and routine was safety, something I craved after the unpredictable fury of the ocean and the ultimate, terrifying unpredictability of loss.

"You mentioned a blow?" Nicki's tone shifted slightly, becoming more professional. "You ran into it then."

"Ran straight through it, I affirmed, the memory raising the phantom vibration of stressed steel. For seven hours, the Atlantic forgot its manners. Walls of water, Gale force winds that screamed through the rigging. We had spray going clear over the bridge! The old girl got a workout, I can tell you." I felt a surge of pride. "But we held fast. My hull groaned, my engines roared, but we kept pushing through. Didn't lose a single plate, barely shipped a drop below decks. My people handled her beautifully."

"Glad to hear it, Ollie," Nicki said sincerely. The playful teasing evaporated when talking about the sea's serious moods. "It pays to be sturdy. That storm... word travels even in port. It makes you think, doesn't it? How quickly things can change out there." There was a pause, a weight in her presence. "Makes you – makes us all – remember how thin the margin is, sometimes."

I knew exactly what she meant. The sea was a fickle mistress. One moment, calm and benevolent, the next, a raging beast. Or worse, a silent, treacherous killer hidden by fog or darkness.

"Speaking of how quickly things can change," Nicki continued, her voice now low and heavy, "you heard about Empress?"

The Empress. Not of the Atlantic lines, but the Empress of Ireland, who worked the Canadian route, sailing the St. Lawrence River. News, especially bad news about one of us, travelled the invisible currents between ships, carried on radio waves and hushed dockside conversations. My grief for Tinny was a constant companion, but news of another disaster, another soul lost to the water, always sent a fresh chill through my hull.

"I did," I replied, the thought chilling me despite the warmth of my engine room. Just whispers at sea, like a cold breath on the surface. "Fog, wasn't it? And a collision?"

"Collision in the fog. Yes," Nicki confirmed, her presence radiating sorrow. "Up the St. Lawrence. She met a collier, the Storstad, early last Friday morning. Thick fog. They saw each other, tried to maneuver, but in the grey blindness... they struck."

She paused, and I felt the collective shiver of the ships around us in the harbor who were listening, sensing the conversation. Docked freighters, ferries moving across the bay, even the smaller coastal steamers seemed to quieten their internal rumbling.

"They struck hard," Nicki continued, her voice tight. "Starboard side amidships. The Storstad's bow went right into her side, between her funnels. A terrible blow. And the worst of it, Ollie... she went down in fourteen minutes. Fourteen minutes from collision to gone."

Fourteen minutes. The number hit me like a physical blow. Fourteen minutes to fight, to launch boats, to scream, to sink. My own sister, Tinny, had lasted longer after hitting the iceberg, though her end was equally inevitable and terrifying, a slow, agonizing surrender over hours compared to the horrific speed of the Empress's demise. But fourteen minutes... that was barely enough time to comprehend the disaster.

"Fourteen minutes," I echoed, the words tasting like salt and fear. "Merciful heavens. She wouldn't have had a chance. Not against a blow like that, in the fog..."

"No chance at all," Nicki confirmed sadly. "Apparently, the water rushed in so fast, she listed terribly almost immediately. Trapped hundreds below decks. Rolled right over onto her side before she slid under. Just... gone."

A low, mournful whistle sounded from a tramp steamer tied up across the way, a rusty, work-worn vessel that had seen its share of close calls. "Fog's a wicked thing," the tramp steamer said "Blind and deaf it makes you. And speed in fog... madness."

A sleek, modern coastal passenger ship, faster than the old tramp, chimed in. "But you have schedules! Passengers demand timeliness! The pressure..."

"Pressure be damned when you can't see the anchor on your own bow," retorted a sturdy harbour tug, its voice gruff but wise. "Better to be late than at the bottom."

"She was a fine ship, Empress," sighed a ferry, its regular back-and-forth across the harbor giving it a perspective on the constant traffic. "Built well, capable. Just... wrong place, wrong time. And the fog."

The collective sorrow settled over us like the harbor mist. We were all steel and power, queens of the waves and workhorses of trade, but against the sheer indifference of the sea, against the blind fury of fog and the unforgiving physics of a sudden impact, we were vulnerable. Built strong, yes, but ultimately fragile.

My own hull felt cold again, the memory of Tinny's fate joining the fresh horror of the Empress of Ireland's. Tinny, struck by ice. Empress, struck by steel. Both lost to the deep, taking so many with them. It was the nightmare we all lived with, the risk we accepted every time we left the safety of port.

"So many souls lost," I murmured, my voice barely audible even to Nicki. "Passengers... crew... their ship soul there, struggling... gone." The image of Empress rolling over, plunging into the cold dark, was agonizing. It brought back the chilling echoes of Tinny's final moments, the desperate struggle, the listing, the plunge.

"They say it was quick, at least for those who made it out," Nicki said, trying, I think, to offer some small comfort. "But the water was freezing, the shock must have been instant for many."

"Better quick than... drawn out," I agreed, thinking of Tinny's long, agonizing hours, the slow descent, the breaking apart. "But was it better? Either way was oblivion."

My focus had to return to the present. We were nearing the pier now. The tugs were nudging me, the lines were being readied by figures on the quay. The noise of the city was growing: people yelling, distant police whistles, the hooves of horses. The living world called.

"I'm almost alongside, Cousin," I told Nicki. "Thank you for telling me the details. It's... hard news, but necessary."

"Always, Ollie," she replied softly. "We are family, after all. We bear witness for each other. We remember."

"We remember," I repeated, the words a vow whispered into the damp air. I would remember Empress, another sister claimed. Just as I would never forget Tinny. Her memory was etched into my very being, a permanent scar in my soul.

I felt a final nudge from a tug, heard the first lines being thrown. The sounds of the harbor enveloped me, the work of arrival demanding my full attention. The grief, the fear, the memory of the storm and the fresh wound of the Empress's loss... they didn't disappear. But they receded, settling back into the quiet, persistent hum beneath my operational awareness. I was Olympic. I had passengers to disembark, cargo to unload, a schedule to keep. I had survived. I had witnessed. And I would continue to sail, carrying my burdens across the waves, always a Queen, always a survivor, always, always, missing my twin. The empty space at the next pier felt vast, and the silence, where Tinny's cheerful greeting should have been, was the loudest sound in the world. But ahead, the work waited. And a ship, even one with a grieving soul, must do her duty.

Chapter 12

The War

- .... . / .—.- .-.

Whispers began, carried on the radio waves like ill winds. Talk of archdukes, of ultimatums, of nations mobilising. At first it felt distant — a European squall far from the broad, predictable highway of the North Atlantic. But the whispers grew louder, more urgent, until they became shouts.

And then, abruptly, the rhythm shattered.

War. August 1914. The word echoed through my steel bones, cold and sharp. The world I knew: elegant voyages, measured rivalries, and the steady cadence of passenger service. They all vanished almost overnight. The sea, once a domain of commerce and travel, transformed into a theatre of war.

My fate was decided swiftly. The White Star Line gave way to the needs of the Admiralty. I was requisitioned, marked for service to the Crown. The vibrant confidence of peacetime was deemed unsuitable for the grey, dangerous world that had dawned.

Dockyard workers swarmed over me, not with the careful hands of decorators and stewards, but with the rough efficiency of war. My funnels lost their proud black tops beneath coats of uniform grey. My bright hull disappeared under drab paint. Brass was dulled, polish abandoned, elegance muted. I became a ghost of my former self — the Grey Ghost.

Luxury gave way to necessity. Staterooms were stripped and filled with tiered bunks. Dining saloons became mess halls crowded with uniforms instead of evening dress. Promenades once alive with leisure now echoed with marching boots and restless waiting.

My purpose shifted utterly. I no longer carried dreams across the Atlantic, but duty. Thousands of young men filled my decks, bound for a continent consumed by fire. Their laughter came in brief bursts, quickly fading into quiet conversations and thoughtful silence. I felt their uncertainty as surely as I felt the sea beneath my keel.

I was still Olympic, but I was becoming something else. I began to see familiar faces changed as I was.

Maury stood beside me again in crowded harbours, her great form painted for war, her lines carrying the quiet confidence of experience. With her was Tania, newly drawn into this harsher world.

"You wear the grey well, Ollie," Maury said, her voice steady despite the transformation we both bore.

"I would rather wear white," I answered. "But we serve where we must."

Tania lingered slightly behind her, watching everything, the soldiers boarding, the armed guards, the constant motion of wartime docks.

"I still feel as though I'm in someone else's role," she admitted. "One moment I was a liner... now they expect me to be a transport. Armed, no less."

"You learn quickly," Maury told her gently. "We all did."

"It does not feel quick," Tania said, almost apologetically.

"It never does at first," I added. "But the sea teaches. It always has."

She seemed to take comfort in that, straightening slightly as another column of troops marched aboard her. Maury watched her with quiet pride; no longer a rival beside me, but an elder sister guiding another through unfamiliar waters.

Not long after, I encountered Lucy.

I expected to see her cloaked in naval grey like the rest of us. Instead, her funnels stood painted black, solemn against her familiar lines.

"You escaped the paint yards," I said.

"Not entirely," she replied, a faint warmth beneath her composure. "But they still need ships to carry passengers. Not soldiers, but families. Diplomats. Those trying to leave before the doors close completely."

"The Atlantic is no longer kind," I warned.

"It never truly was," Lucy said softly. "We simply pretended otherwise."

There was courage in her decision, a quieter kind than ours, but no less real.

"Safe sailing, Lucy."

"And to you, Ollie," she answered. "Bring them there and bring yourself back."

We parted soon after, each bound for different duties beneath the same darkening sky.

Days later, I searched the horizon for Britt, expecting grey paint or altered company colours.

Instead, she appeared brilliant against the sea: white hull gleaming, orange funnels bright, green bands and red crosses marking her unmistakably.

For a moment, I scarcely recognised her.

"Britt?" I asked, astonished.

Her reply carried a calm I had not heard before. "Yes. They've given me a different duty."

"A hospital ship," I said, understanding slowly.

She sounded almost relieved. "I will carry the wounded. Bring them away from the fighting instead of toward it."

The pride in her voice was quiet, grounded.

"It suits you," I told her.

"I think so," she said. "It feels… right. A way to show mercy. For all of them. For Tinny, too."

At that, I felt something steady settle within me. She was no longer the unfinished younger sister I remembered from the yards. War had not hardened her, it had clarified her.

"You have grown, Britt."

There was a small pause before she answered, warm and certain. "I learned from my sisters."

And I realised she truly had.

War changed even the way we moved upon the sea. Zigzag manoeuvres became our new language, patterns meant to confuse the unseen hunters below.

Maury adapted quickly.

"Think of it as a dance," she told Tania during one shared exercise. "An inelegant one, perhaps."

"I was built for straight lines," Tania protested as she corrected another turn.

"So were we all," I said. "But survival rarely is."

At first her movements lagged, hesitant and uneven. Yet voyage by voyage she improved, until her turns grew confident, purposeful, no longer imitation, but mastery.

The Atlantic itself felt altered. Competition and record runs became distant memories. Speed was now survival. Every ripple might conceal danger; every shadow might hide a periscope. Lookouts searched not for ice, but for death rising silently from below.

The Great War reshaped us all.

I was no longer simply a queen of the Atlantic, but a warhorse, and I was not alone. Ships that had once been rivals now shared the same burden, the same vigilance, the same responsibility for the lives entrusted to us.

In peacetime, Maury and I had measured ourselves against one another in miles and hours. In war, those rivalries faded into something quieter and stronger. We met in crowded ports and grey anchorages, comrades rather than competitors, sisters bound not by speed but by service.

We had entered a darker ocean together, and together, we learned how to endure it.

Then came the strike that sent a chill through my iron plates, colder than any North Atlantic ice.

It was 1915. While Maury and I carried troops and supplies beneath constant watch for the unseen threat below, Lucy remained in passenger service — fast, proud, still carrying civilians, families, and fragile pieces of normal life across a world already breaking apart.

The news arrived like a physical blow, spreading through the docks in hushed voices and stunned silence.

Lucy had been sunk.

Not by storm.

Not by ice.

But by a torpedo, fired deliberately by a German U-boat off the coast of Ireland.

The harbour itself seemed to fall still.

I felt the loss deeply; the absence of a familiar presence upon the sea, an emptiness where certainty had once existed. My thoughts drifted unbidden to that terrible spring three years earlier, when Tinny had vanished beneath the Atlantic. I knew the shape of that silence. I knew how loudly absence could echo.

But Maury's grief was different.

I had already seen it: sharp and blazing, striking outward like lightning. Anger directed at the sea itself, at fate, at the unseen enemy beneath the waves. Words spoken in fury that neither of us truly meant. When we parted that day, she had wanted only solitude, and I had left her to it.

For several days afterward, we did not speak.

Then, one grey morning in harbour, I felt her presence approach.

She came alongside quietly, without the usual confidence that defined her movements. For a long moment she said nothing.

"Ollie," she finally began, her voice subdued. "I was... harsh before."

I hesitated, unsure how to answer.

"You had reason," I said gently.

"No." A pause followed, heavy but controlled. "I had anger. There is a difference."

The water lapped softly between us.

"I should not have turned it toward you."

"There is nothing to forgive," I told her. "Grief rarely arrives calmly."

She let out a long, slow vibration, not quite a sigh, but close.

"It is iron and blood now," she said quietly.

The words settled heavily between us. Not shouted this time. Simply stated, as fact.

I searched for something that might comfort her, something drawn from my own past.

"The sea remembers," I said at last.

She did not flare with anger as before. Instead, she gave a tired, almost hollow reply.

"I know you believe that."

Another silence followed, not hostile, only weary.

"I keep thinking," she continued, "she tried to hold on. Lucy always was stubborn. Strong." Her voice faltered slightly. "But the damage was too much."

The grief beneath her restraint trembled through the water.

"She died alone."

The words carried more weight than any storm.

"I am sorry," I said, knowing how small the words sounded.

"So am I," Maury replied softly. "Sorry I could not reach her. Sorry I could do nothing at all."

I understood that feeling too well — the endless questioning, the impossible desire to change what had already passed beyond reach.

After a while she spoke again, quieter still.

"When Tinny was lost... how did you continue?"

I turned inward, toward memories I rarely allowed myself to revisit.

"I did not know how," I admitted. "I simply kept moving. There were still people who needed passage. Crews who depended on me. Standing was the only thing I could do."

Maury absorbed that in silence.

"The anger is still there," she confessed. "It feels... wrong that it should fade."

"It does not fade," I said. "It changes shape."

She considered that for a long time.

"At sea," she said slowly, "we endure storms because we must. Not because we accept them."

"Yes," I answered. "Exactly."

The tension between us eased then, replaced not by comfort, but by understanding.

We remained together in quiet companionship, two great liners resting side by side, sharing the weight of a loss neither could undo. She spoke occasionally of Lucy, small details only a twin would remember: the subtle difference in engine rhythm, the tone of her whistle, the way she carried speed with effortless pride.

I listened.

Gradually, the sharp edge of her fury softened into something steadier, not peace, but resolve.

From that day forward, our bond changed. The old rivalry meant little beside what we now carried. We were no longer competitors of the Atlantic run, but survivors of the same war, sisters shaped by the same wounds.

And together, we returned to sea, zigging and zagging across hostile waters, carrying not only soldiers, but the memory of the one who no longer sailed beside us.

From then on, our bond deepened immeasurably. The old White Star and Cunard banners still flew, but between Maury and me, they were just colours. We were two ships scarred by loss, united by service in a brutal time. We looked out for each other. When we were in the same convoy, I felt her presence like a comforting anchor, and I knew she felt mine. Her speed was her weapon, mine was my resilience, my size, my ability to absorb punishment.

I remember one particularly tense crossing later in the war, the air thick with the reported presence of U-boats. The convoy scattered at a signal, everyone turning away from a suspected threat. I saw Maury, a greyhound fading into the mist with her characteristic surge of speed. And I, the elder, steadier sister, held my course, or turned deliberately towards the suspected danger, sometimes even hoping for a confrontation.

She never truly got over losing her twin, how could she? The bond between them was unique. But the shared grief, the understanding that some losses are inflicted with deliberate cruelty while others are the result of indifferent fate, forged a steel link between us that lasted long after the war ended and we returned, briefly, to our civilian roles. We were the survivors, the sisters who had carried the weight of the world on our decks and the pain of lost siblings in our hearts. We had faced the storm, felt the sting of malice and the cold indifference of nature, and we had endured, carrying a silent, profound understanding of each other's enduring scars. And sometimes, in the quiet hours at sea, I would feel her presence on the horizon, a fellow spirit who knew the true, heavy cost of the waves we sailed.

Chapter 13

The Survivor

- .... . / ... ..- .-. ...- .. ...- -—.-.

The salt spray was a familiar sting against my steel plates, a sensation I'd known since the first time I tasted the open sea. But on that crisp morning, nestled alongside the dock in her immaculate white paint and red crosses, and those, admittedly, gaudy crane davits, my sister Britt felt different. Lighter, somehow, despite the looming presence of her orange funnels against the grey sky. I, however, was painted in the "razzle dazzle" colors as humans called it. Bloody clown suit was my name for it.

"You look... ready, Britt," I rumbled, my voice a low thrumming through the water that separated us. My own hull, bearing the scars and grimier hues of troop transport, felt heavy and weathered in comparison.

She shifted slightly, a gentle settling at her moorings. I could feel her presence, a quiet strength emanating from her vast form. "As ready as I can be, Ollie," she replied, her voice softer, a little hesitant. "They've finished the conversion. All the sterile spaces, the operating theatres, the beds..." She trailed off. "It feels like a calling, this work. A purpose, beyond just crossing the Atlantic."

"It is a noble purpose," I assured her. "To bring healing in a time of so much hurt." The Great War. It had changed everything. Our lives of luxury crossings, of carrying the hopeful and the wealthy, were a distant dream. Now, we were instruments of conflict, or in Britt's case, its grim aftermath.

We fell silent for a moment, the air thick with unspoken memories and the weight of the present. It was impossible not to think of her. Our beautiful, grand sister, Tinny. Her name was a ghost between us, a chilling reminder of the sea's indifference and the fragility of even the mightiest creations of man.

"Do you ever...?" Britt started, then stopped. I knew what she meant. Did I ever replay that night? Did I ever feel the cold shock, the impossible angle she must have taken, the sounds of her end? Always. She was the first great blow. A rending in the very fabric of our family.

"Every time the ice flows creep south," I admitted, my bow feeling a familiar ache. "Every time the fog rolls in thick. She was... taken from us. So suddenly. So unfairly."

"And Lucy," Britt added, her voice low, edged with sorrow. "Torpedoed. Just like that. Gone. Maury is still reeling, you know. Losing a twin...It makes this feel... heavier," Britt confessed. "Carrying so many vulnerable souls now. Not passengers seeking new lives, but soldiers broken and bleeding. I have to get them back. Safely. After Tinny, after what happened to dear Lucy... I feel this huge weight. To carry on a good legacy. To prove our class isn't just about size, but about service. About enduring."

She had matured so much, I couldn't believe it. From the cocky unfinished ship still high and dry, to this introspective and sympathetic servant of the Crown. I felt such pride and love for her. Still, her words resonated deeply within me. I understood that burden. As the eldest surviving sister, much of that weight had fallen on my broad decks initially. I had to show that the 'Olympic' class hadn't been a mistake, that we weren't cursed. I'd continued the Atlantic runs, then taken on the grim task of troop transport. It was hard, relentless work, dodging shadows, feeling the vibration of distant depth charges, the constant awareness of danger.

"You will carry a good legacy, Britt," I told her, projecting as much steady confidence as I could muster. "Protecting the wounded, bringing them home... there is nothing more honourable. You have the strength for it. We are built tough, remember? Built to weather storms. I proved that two years ago."

She was quiet again for a moment, and I felt a sense of peace settle between us, a quiet comfort in shared understanding. "Be safe out there, Ollie," she finally said. "The Channel, the Western Approaches... they say the U-boats are everywhere."

"You too, Britt," I replied. "The Mediterranean can be just as treacherous. Fair winds and following seas, sister."

She gave me a sly smile, "Don't smudge your clown suit."

"Oh right," I chuckled, "Wouldn't want to mess that up."

Soon after, her tugs nudged her away, and she began her slow, stately journey out of the harbor, her white hull a stark, hopeful shape against the grey backdrop. I watched her go until she was just a smudge on the horizon, a brave vessel sailing towards her destiny.

Then, my own orders came. Sail to Nova Scotia, pickup a load of soldiers, then another dark, urgent dash across the waves to some embattled shore. The rhythm of war transport settled over me: the controlled chaos of loading, the tense hours at sea, the fleeting moments of relief in a foreign port, and the relentless return journey.

My voyages were demanding. I learned to smell the sea differently, to feel the subtle changes in current that might signal danger. I learned the silent language of escort destroyers and the heart-stopping moment when a periscope was spotted, sending us all into zigzagging, nerve-wracking evasive maneuvers.

Through it all, my thoughts would often turn to Britt. Was she safe? Was her mission going well? I heard snippets of news in port – whispers from other vessels, the dockworkers' talk. "The big hospital ship... doing good work down south...." It filled me with pride. She was upholding our name, our class.

We met by chance, though in wartime nothing ever truly felt accidental.

I had just completed another crossing, another endless procession of soldiers carried safely from one shore to another, another departure that felt identical to the last. Southampton lay under a low grey sky, cranes creaking, whistles echoing without enthusiasm. Duty waited again, already preparing to begin anew.

I expected only a brief greeting when I recognised Britt's bright white hull across the harbour.

She stood apart from the grey ships like a fragment of another world: white paint marked with green bands and red crosses, her funnels warm with colour where the rest of us had faded into war.

For a while, neither of us spoke.

"You look tired," she said at last.

I almost laughed at that. "Ships are not meant to look tired."

"And yet," she replied gently, "you do."

The honesty of it slipped past my usual composure

"It never ends," I admitted. "Crossing after crossing. Load, sail, unload, return. Thousands aboard, thousands gone again. I used to measure voyages in seasons... now they blur together." I hesitated before adding quietly, "Sometimes I wonder if any of it changes anything at all."

The words felt strange once spoken; thoughts I had carried alone for far too long.

Britt did not answer immediately.

"I envy you," she said instead.

That startled me. "Me?" "You carry them forward," she said. "You deliver them alive. They leave your decks cheering sometimes."

Her voice softened.

"They do not cheer when they leave mine."

I felt the weight behind her words then something she rarely allowed anyone to see.

"I thought... this duty suited you," I said carefully. "You seemed so certain."

"I am certain," she answered. "That does not make it easy."

A long pause followed, filled only by the slow movement of harbour water.

"They bring them to me broken," Britt continued quietly. "Some grateful. Some frightened. Some already fading before we even leave port. I tell Tania to focus on the ones we can help. I tell her not to lose heart." She faltered slightly. "But sometimes I feel like I am asking her to learn a strength I am still pretending to have."

The admission hung between us, fragile. "I thought you never doubted," I said.

She gave a faint, almost embarrassed vibration of amusement. "You always were the strong one, Ollie."

I nearly protested. then stopped.

"No," I said softly. "After Tinny... they rebuilt me. Strengthened me. Everyone said I was safer, better, proven." I hesitated. "But I never stopped wondering if I had failed first. If I should have been stronger before."

The old insecurity surfaced more easily than I expected.

"You were never questioned," I added before I could stop myself. "You were new. Untouched by that shadow."

Britt was silent for several moments.

"I envied you," she said again, more firmly this time.

I turned my attention fully toward her.

"You endured it," she continued. "You survived losing her and kept sailing. You carried people afterward. You proved ships like us could continue." Her voice trembled faintly. "I feel as though no matter how many I help... it never balances what we lost."

The harbour noises faded into the background as the truth settled between us.

"You think your duty is not enough," I said.

"And you think yours has no end," she replied gently.

We both fell quiet at that, recognising the symmetry neither of us had seen before."I sometimes wish," she admitted carefully, "that my work ended when they disembarked. That I did not have to watch them slip away." "And I sometimes wish," I answered, "that I knew what became of those I carry. Whether any of it mattered."

The confession felt almost like relief.

For the first time since the war began, neither of us was trying to be the stronger sister.

Just sisters.

After a while Britt spoke again, softer.

"Do you remember how proud Tinny was of us both?"

I did. The memory rose easily, bright, uncomplicated, untouched by war.

"She believed we each had our own purpose," Britt said. "Not the same one."

I considered that.

"You carry hope forward," she continued. "I carry it back."

The simplicity of it eased something inside me I had not realised was strained.

"And neither of us is meant to do both," I said.

She seemed to settle at that, the tension in her presence loosening.

We remained together a while longer, saying little, sharing only the quiet understanding that came from finally admitting weakness without judgment.

Soon enough, duty would call us apart again, soldiers waiting for me, wounded waiting for her, but for that brief harbour evening, the war felt slightly less endless.

And when we parted, I no longer felt alone in it.

Months passed. The war ground on, a hungry beast devouring ships and lives. I completed successful runs, carrying men and supplies, bringing back the wounded and the weary. Each return to a home port was a small victory, a breath of temporary safety before the next assignment.

And then, I came back to Southampton. It had been a particularly arduous run, filled with close calls and constant tension. I was weary, my plates humming with fatigue, my funnels grimy with the effort of pushing through rough seas. But I felt the familiar surge of anticipation. Perhaps Britt would be here. Perhaps I would see her gleaming white hull, hear her gentle voice.

I docked in my usual spot, the ropes secured, the gangways lowered. The immediate flurry of activity around me began – cargo unloading, shore leave for the men. But for a moment, I was still, scanning the familiar lines of the harbor.

She wasn't here.

A cold knot formed deep within my engineering spaces. Unreasonable, perhaps. The seas were vast; our paths wouldn't always cross. But the absence felt too large, too heavy. I strained my senses, trying to feel her presence in the water, in the air.

Nothing.

Other ships were in port – grey warships, tired freighters, the occasional liner pressed into service like myself. And there, across the busy waterway, I saw her. Maury. Still serving, still mourning.

She looked... aged. Not just the wear and tear of war service, but a deep, etched sorrow that no amount of paint could cover. Her familiar jaunty lines seemed stooped, her funnels seemed to sigh rather than stand proud.

Slowly, deliberately, she began to move, crossing the distance towards my berth. My unease sharpened into dread. Ships in port, especially those from different lines, didn't usually just... visit. Not unless there was important news. And given who she was, and who wasn't here...

She drew alongside my mooring, her engines falling silent. Her great hull loomed near mine, a shared sorrow passing between us like a chilling current.

"Ollie," she said, her voice a low, mournful note that scraped against my very soul. It was full of the pain of her own great loss, a pain that made her the perfect, terrible messenger.

"Maury," I managed, my voice tight. "What is it? Britt... Britannic... is she...?"

Maury vibrated with a deep sigh that seemed to come from her very keel. "Oh, Ollie. My dear girl." The compassion in her tone was overwhelming, but it did nothing to soften the blow I knew was coming. "She's gone."

The world tilted. No. Gone. Like Titanic? Like Lusitania? The word was a physical impact.

"How?" I whispered, the sound barely audible above the harbor noise. "Was it...?"

"A mine," Mauretania confirmed, her voice thick with sympathy. "In the Aegean Sea. A German mine. It happened last month. November."

November. It was December now. I hadn't even known. The vastness of the war, the distances, had kept me ignorant while my sister met her end.

"Was it... quick?" I asked, needing details, needing to understand the manner of her destruction.

"Relatively," Mauretania said softly. "She went down fast, they said. About an hour. But... there is some small comfort, Olympic. Most of the souls aboard were saved. Her boats were launched. The sea was calm. Her purpose, her noble work... she saw to it that as many as possible survived. I heard she fought hard to stay afloat, to try and beach herself. She did build that good legacy she wanted."

Most survived. But Britt didn't. The ship, the soul, the steel and steam that was my vibrant sister – she was gone. Lying on the seabed in a foreign sea.

Tears, hot and impossible for a ship built of iron and steel, seemed to sting my anchor chains. Two of us now. Sunk. One by nature's brutal chance, the other by man's deliberate destruction. The 'Wonderful Trio' was broken, shattered irrevocably.

Maury was silent for a long moment, letting the news sink into my very structure. Then she spoke again, her voice gentle. "I know this pain, Ollie. Losing a sister. Losing her this way... it tears a hole in you that never quite closes. Lucy... she was my reflection. And now... you carry the weight for all three of you. The legacy of your class. The sole survivor of your magnificent sisters."

I looked at her, at the twin who understood what it meant to have half of yourself ripped away. She carried her grief with a quiet dignity that was both heartbreaking and inspiring.

"Two sisters," I finally murmured, the words heavy in the air. "Both gone. In different ways, but both gone."

"You remain," Maury said, her presence a solid, comforting anchor in my sudden storm of grief. "You carry their memory. You carry the thousands you have saved and transported. You are Olympic. The Reliable."

Reliable. A name I had worn with pride. Now it felt like a burden, the burden of being the last one standing. The harbor sounds seemed distant, muted. The hustle of the docks felt alien. All I could feel was the gaping emptiness where Britt's presence should have been, the cold knowledge that she was gone forever.

The war raged on around us, heedless of my personal sorrow. Other ships came and went, their missions urgent. But for me, the port had changed. It was a place marked by absence, a reminder of what had been lost.

I stood there for a long time, with Maury silent beside me, two great ships bearing the invisible wounds of a devastating war, two sisters in survival and sorrow. The sea, stretching out beyond the harbor mouth, seemed vast and indifferent, the keeper of so many secrets, the builder and the destroyer of dreams. And I, the last of the trio, had to face it again, carrying not just the weight of my cargo, but the immeasurable weight of my lost sisters. My work was not done. It could never be done, not as long as I floated. I was Olympic. I was the survivor. And I would carry on.

Chapter 14

The Ram

- .... . / .-. .- —

The grey, bruised sea was my constant companion in these days. Not the vibrant, deep blue of peacetime crossings, but a churning, watchful grey that mirrored the mood of the world. It was the year 1918, and the Great War had sunk its claws deep into the flesh of the Earth and the souls of her ships. I felt the weight of every lost vessel, every drowned soul, as if my own hull were leaking.

I had sailed the Channel countless times, but never with the knot of tension that now coiled in my gut with each revolution of my screws. Gone were the grand promenades, the laughter echoing through my stairwells, the thrill of the transatlantic dash. Now, my purpose was grim: carrying troops, supplies, the implements of destruction, across waters thick with unseen menace.

This day, I was eastbound in the English Channel, painted in a new version of what the humans called "razzle dazzle," though to me it was a clown suit compared to my former grandeur. But I was cutting a determined path through the choppy water. Above, the sky was a low ceiling of cloud, pressing down on the world. My escorts, nimble little destroyers, darted like anxious terriers at my flanks, their presence a small comfort against the pervasive fear. My decks were crowded, not with eager tourists, but with khaki-clad young American men, their faces a mix of apprehension and forced bravado.

The routine was a monotonous, nerve-wracking waltz: scan the horizon, feel the shudder of distant depth charges – was that for us? – and push on, always push on.

My Captain, Bertram Hayes, the steady, weathered soul who shared my bridge, had eyes that missed nothing. He was my eyes, my ears, my connection to the immediate world beyond my steel skin. I felt his vigilance like a physical extension of my own being.

A shout cut through the wind's howl. From the bridge, it was relayed down through my structure like a galvanic shock.

"Periscope! Bearing two-six-zero! Two points off the port bow!"

My systems flared with immediate, cold dread. A U-boat. The hunter of my kind. The killer of Lucy. The killer of countless others. It was there, a barely visible sliver disturbing the surface, a venomous eye watching me, me.

The air became thick with adrenaline. Below, the thrum of my engines, usually a comforting pulse, now felt urgent, strained. On my forward deck, men scrambled to the guns I now carried, weapons of defiance bolted onto my grand structure.

"Open fire!"

I felt the command reverberate through me, a fierce jolt. Then, the answering crack! and roar! from my deck guns. The sound was alien, brutal, mounted on me. Shells screamed away, splashing near the periscope, geysers erupting from the grey sea.

The periscope vanished. It wasn't hit, not directly, but it was diving. Trying to escape my wrath, to slip beneath the waves and prepare its deadly strike.

A cold, hard resolve settled over me, unlike anything I had felt before. Not just the fear of the hunted, but the coiled fury of the grieving, of the wronged survivors. Tinny, Lucy, Britt... their faces swam before my internal vision, spectral and accusing.

From the bridge, the Captain's voice, tight with adrenaline but clear and decisive, cut through the sounds of my labouring engines and the distant splashes. "He's diving! He'll try to get under us! Full speed! Give me everything! Hard a-starboard! Ram him! Ram him!"

The thrill that shot through me was electric, terrifying, and exhilarating. Ram him. Not just avoid, not just defend, but attack. Use my immense mass, my speed, my very being as a weapon.

My engines responded, the turbine whined, pushing my screws to their absolute limit. I felt the immense power surge through my shafts, my hull quivering with the strain. I swung hard to starboard, my massive frame leaning into the turn, the sea boiling around me. My bow cut through the water with savage intent, aiming for the place where the periscope had vanished, where I knew the steel predator lurked below.

My intention was clear, etched into the very heart of my being in that moment. I wanted to catch him on my starboard side. To drag his miserable, cruel hull along the steel that had been crippled and then made whole again through my sister's sacrifice. To feel the victory on that side, to dedicate the vengeance to her, to Tinny, whose sacrifice had made my continued existence possible.

I leaned into the turn, my forward momentum carrying me inexorably towards the U-boat's estimated position. The surface was churning, my massive bow throwing up spray as I bore down.

Then, I felt him. A solid, jarring thump deep below my waterline, forward. The U-boat. I had him. My bow was over him, his steel skin scraping against my own. It was a terrible, beautiful sound, the sound of the hunter becoming the hunted.

But the sea, and my own considerable momentum, had a cruel sense of humour. I was leaning hard to starboard, straining to keep him there, to drag him along that side. But the submarine, struck at an angle, angled by the force of my turn, didn't stay obediently pinned to my starboard flank.

With a sickening lurch that ran the entire length of my keel, I felt him slide. Not to the starboard, where I wanted him, where the ghosts of my past waited, but across my underside. Past my bilges, toward the massive, churning shapes of my three great propellers. My stomach twisted with a sudden, cold premonition.

He slid, scraping and protesting, towards my port side. Towards that propeller that drove me forward with relentless power.

The sound was unimaginable. Not a scrape, but a terrible, rending shriek of tortured metal. My port propeller, a colossal screw of bronze, spinning at full speed, met the unforgiving steel of the U-boat's hull. My blades, designed to drive me through the waves with speed and grace, became instruments of brutal dissection. I felt the impact rattle through my entire structure, a violent shudder that seemed to loosen every rivet. It was not a clean cut, but a tearing, a grinding, a catastrophic mutilation below the surface.

The U-boat's scream, a sound of metal death, was brief and final. The scraping stopped. The shuddering eased. There was a sudden, almost unnerving silence below, replaced only by the roar of my own engines and the rush of water past my hull.

I had done it. I had rammed and sunk a U-boat. Technically, the only merchant vessel in history to do so.

I continued my turn, completing a wide circle. The sea where the U-boat had been was now marked by a dark, spreading slick of oil, mixed with debris. And amidst the flotsam, I saw them. Men. Struggling in the cold water, surrounded by the death of their vessel.

There were many of them, clinging to wreckage. I counted them – or rather, my Captain's eyes counted them and the number filtered to me – thirty-five. Men who had been moments ago bent on my destruction, on the destruction of the soldiers I carried.

My orders were absolute. My mission paramount. I could not stop. I dared not stop. To linger was to invite another attack, to risk the lives of thousands aboard me. To stop for enemy sailors, no matter their plight, was unthinkable in the brutal calculus of wartime. Not for me. Not with this cargo.

We sailed on. My bow, though unmarked, felt heavy. My hull still vibrated with the memory of that terrible impact, that grinding shriek of destruction.

And I felt it – the fierce, primal surge. Vengeance. Justice. For Lucy, torpedoed and helpless. For Britt, mined unsuspecting. Even, in a strange, circular way, for Tinny, whose life was cut short by the indifferent sea that was now stained with the oil of her killer's brethren.

I had struck back. I, the grand old lady of the sea, had become a weapon, a ram. The thrill was intoxicating, a release of years of simmering grief and anger.

But beneath the triumph, a different feeling gnawed at me. A bitter twist of irony. I had wanted to use the starboard side. The side that bore the phantom wound of my sister's sacrifice. To feel the U-boat's death throes against the steel bought with her life. To redeem that side, somehow.

Instead, I had used the port. The propeller that had sliced through steel and bone belonged to the other side. The side that was whole, untouched by that particular history. The side that now carried... what? Guilt? A different kind of scar?

The images stayed with me as I steamed on. The dark oil slick. The faces in the water, shrinking into the distance. The terrible sound of that propeller tearing flesh and steel. And the phantom ache on my starboard side, the side that wished it had been the instrument of justice, but remained empty, a silent monument to a different loss.

My engines continued their steady beat, a rhythm of survival, of duty. But now, beneath the sound, I heard the echo of a shriek and the quiet lament of a propeller that had done its duty, yes, but not with the grace or the vengeance I had intended for it. The war left scars in unexpected places, and sometimes, even victory felt heavy with sorrow and regret. I sailed on, carrying my passengers towards their destiny and adding another layer of complex, unresolvable history to my soul.

Chapter 15

The Talk

- .... . / - .- .- .. -.-

I felt the familiar thrum beneath my keel, the heavy, shuffling weight spreading across my tired decks. Soldiers again. Thousands of them, young faces etched with a mixture of nerves and forced bravado, their boots pounding a steady rhythm that echoed not just through my steel bones, but deep within my soul. It was the summer of 1918, and the war felt like a relentless tide, forever washing fresh waves of humanity onto my back, carrying them away to places few ever fully returned from.

I lay alongside Maury, Her vibrant civilian colours were long gone, replaced by the same blasted clown suit I wore. She was taking on her own cargo of hopes and fears on the adjacent pier. I could feel her presence, a warmth in the cold harbour air that went beyond mere proximity. We understood each other, we great liners turned troopers, the silent witnesses to so much sorrow and steel.

"Rough day, Ollie?"

I settled deeper into my berth, the mooring lines groaning softly in response. "Just the usual, Maury. Loading up. Feels heavier every time, somehow."

"Tell me about it," she said, her voice a deep, steady current. "Saw one young lad trip on the gangplank just now. Scared stiff, poor thing. Makes your plates ache just watching them."

"Aye. And seeing their families on the quay..." The image brought a familiar pang. The waving hands, the tear-streaked faces, the unspoken prayers cast out across the water, hoping we would carry their loved ones safely through the dangers that lurked unseen.

We fell silent for a moment, the noise of the docks filling the space between our thoughts – the shouts of officers, the rumble of carts, the endless tramp of boots. There was a shared weariness between us, a knowledge of the terrible things we had witnessed, the friends we had lost. Other ships, gone in a flash of fire or a slow, agonizing groan into the dark waters.

"Heard you had a bit of excitement a while back," Maury said, her tone shifting, a spark of something fierce in her voice. "Down in the Channel, wasn't it? Word gets around, even here."

I felt a shiver run through my hull, not of cold, but of memory. The image flashed behind my eyes – the grey water, the sudden, dark shape. "Aye, that was me. About six months ago now."

"They said you got one," Maury pressed, her voice full of hard satisfaction. "A U-boat."

"I did." The admission hung in the air, heavy and complex.

"Bloody hell, Ollie! Good for you!" Her pleasure was palpable, a wave of righteous fury turned into triumph. "Justice, eh? For all they've done. For Lucy..." Her voice trailed off, the old wound still raw. "For Britt."

"Justice, maybe," I echoed, but the word felt hollow, like a bent scrap of metal. "It wasn't... clean."

"Clean?" Maury's confusion was evident. "Bloody hell, Ollie, they sneak under the water, they fire without warning, they leave no trace but wreckage and bodies. What's clean about any of it? You stopped one! That's all that matters!"

"I saw it there," I began, the memory unfolding like a dark stain. "Convoy was steaming steady. Grey day, bit of chop. I was just holding my course, watching the destroyers darting about like angry terriers. And then... I saw the periscope. Just a ripple, a brief glint."

I paused, feeling the tension of that moment flood back. "The sudden, cold certainty that gripped me. It was close. Too close. No time for signals, no time for the escorts to react. Not if I wanted to save the ships around me, and myself."

"So you went for it," Maury finished, her voice hushed with understanding.

"Aye. The decision wasn't made in my bridge, not really. It was made in my soul, a surge of pure, burning rage fueled by the ghosts of torpedoed friends and mined sisters. I turned sharp, put on a burst of speed. Aimed straight for where I'd seen it disappear beneath the waves."

I remembered the groan deep within me as my rudder swung hard, the sudden lurch as my engines roared, driving my massive bulk forward with desperate speed. The water creamed away from my bow as I bore down on the hidden threat.

"And then?" Maury urged.

"I felt the impact. It wasn't loud, not like a collision topside. It was a deep, grinding crunch absorbed into the vastness of my hull, a tearing sound far below the surface. Felt it shudder right through me. Like running over a tin can with a steamroller."

"You hit it!" Maury exclaimed, excitement rising again.

"Aye. Felt it crumple beneath my forepeak. Knew I'd broken its back. But that wasn't the worst part. As I passed over," I continued, my voice dropping, the memory turning bitter, "my propellers were turning, still driving me forward. And the port one..."

I felt a phantom vibration pulse through my side, the side that faced the dock now, the side away from the open sea. The side that usually felt the comforting rub of a pier or the gentle sway of calm waters.

"My port propeller, the massive screw on my left side, it... it caught it."

The sound was still burned into my memory, a sound that still echoed in the quiet corners of my soul when the nights were long. "There was a shriek. Metal on metal, tearing, ripping, a final, agonizing scream from the U-boat as my huge blades sliced through its pressure hull like a knife through butter. Felt the vibration of it, heard the awful sound singing up my shaft, through my stern, into my very being."

Silence fell between us again, thick and heavy, punctuated only by the distant harbour sounds. Maury seemed to absorb the brutal detail, processing the clinical violence of it.

"So you... you sliced it in half? With your prop?" Her voice was awed, a hint of morbid fascination. "Bloody hell, Ollie. That's... that's something."

"It sank immediately, of course." I felt a cold detachment as I spoke, the same I had felt in that moment. "Just a swirl of oil and debris where it had been."

"And the crew?" Maury asked, though she likely knew the answer.

"Some came up," I admitted, the worst of the memory surfacing now. "Scrambling out of the hatches and holes, into the wreckage. Faces in the water... looking up at me."

I had seen those faces for months afterward, whenever I closed my eyes, whenever the water grew dark around me. Desperate, terrified, pleading eyes. Eyes that had seen the grey underside of my vast hull looming above them, felt the terrible power of my engine driving my propeller through their world.

"I... I kept going." The admission was hard. "Had the convoy to consider. Couldn't stop. Had to maintain speed, course. Left them there. Left them to the cold Channel swell. Left them to whatever fate found them amongst the wreckage of their own vessel."

Maury was quiet for a long moment. "You did what you had to do, Ollie," she finally said, her voice soft but firm. "It's war. You can't... you can't stop for survivors from a U-boat. Not after what they do. Every one of them is a threat."

"I know," I whispered, the logic cold and uncomforting. "But still... the faces."

"The faces fade eventually," she said with a hint of the old salt's pragmatism born of too much experience. "Or you learn to lock them away. You saved lives, Ollie. Thousands of lives in that convoy. Don't forget that. And probably stopped more deaths after that."

"It's not just that," I confessed, the real source of my disquiet finally surfacing. "It's... how it happened."

"How do you mean?"

"The prop, Maury." I focused on the heavy, powerful quadrant on my port side. "It was the port one."

Again, silence. Maury seemed to ponder this, the meaning I was trying to convey.

"Ollie... it's just a propeller. It's on your left side."

"But that's just it!" I felt a surge of frustrated anguish. "Lucy went down on her starboard side! Britt was struck on her starboard side! And Tinny... my sister... my beautiful, lost Titanic... she was torn open by that iceberg on her starboard side!"

The memory of that night, the icy grip of the berg, the tearing steel, the agonizing list to starboard before she slipped beneath the waves – it was a wound that never truly healed. Her sacrifice, her loss, was forever linked to that side of my family, that side of our hulls.

"And the Empress. I know she wasn't part of our family, but she was struck on her starboard side. All the pain, all the loss... it's on the starboard," I explained, the words tumbling out, trying to articulate a feeling that defied simple logic but felt profoundly true to my ship's soul. "That's the side where the danger found us, where the ocean claimed its price. Titanic's legacy is on my starboard side, in that phantom tearing sensation I sometimes feel when the sea is rough. The side that suffered."

"And you sank the U-boat with your port prop," Maury finished for me, her voice quiet with dawning understanding.

"Yes!" I felt the frustration build. "It wasn't... it wasn't done by the side that remembered Tinny's sacrifice! It wasn't vengeance struck with the wounded flank! It was done with the other side, the side that was untouched by that specific kind of loss. It feels... wrong. Brutal, yes, effective, yes... but tainted. Like I used the wrong hand to strike the blow. It should have been the starboard! The side that carries the memory!"

I paused, the absurdity of it weighing on me, yet the feeling was stubbornly real. "It feels like I used cold efficiency, the untouched side, instead of righteous fury from the side that remembers the iceberg, the torpedo, the mine. Does that make any sense?"

Maury was silent for a longer time this time, processing the strange, deep-seated symbolism I was wrestling with. The souls of ships, I suppose, felt things in ways humans couldn't fully grasp. Our bodies were our homes, our identities; every scar, every modification, every side, had meaning.

"Yes, Ollie," she finally murmured, her voice filled with unexpected empathy. "I think I do. It's like... you feel like the act wasn't connected to the pain? Like it was just... killing?"

"Exactly!" Relief washed over me that she understood. "It wasn't redemption through sacrifice's memory. It was just... crushing something with the other side. And that shriek, Maury... the shriek of the prop tearing metal... it wasn't a cry of triumph. It sounded like... like breaking something sacred."

"Oh, love," Maury said, her voice the warmest I had heard it in years. "Look, I get the starboard thing. Believe me, losing Lucy the way I did... that scar is deep. And seeing Britt go down... I know that feeling of loss on that side. But Ollie..." she paused, choosing her words carefully. "That U-boat was a threat to your whole self! Not just your starboard! It could have hit you anywhere, could have hit any ship in that convoy. Your port side... it defended you! It defended all of you!

"It didn't matter which propeller did the job," she insisted gently. "It mattered that the job was done. That you took out a threat. Maybe... maybe the port side needed to step up precisely because the starboard carried such a heavy burden. Maybe it was your port side protecting your starboard, protecting the memory, protecting the future."

I considered this. My port side protecting my starboard? The untouched side fighting for the side that had suffered so much? It was a different way of looking at it. Less about symbolic vengeance, more about inherent self-preservation and protection of the collective.

"Think of it like this, Ollie," Maury continued, her tone practical again, like one soldier advising another on how to carry their pack. "Those faces... yeah, they'll stay with you. That sound... probably will too. War does that. Leaves marks you can't paint over. But you were there. You fought back. And you won that fight. With everything you had, starboard and port."

I knew she was right. It wasn't just about vengeance for the fallen; it was about survival for the living. And in that moment, driven by a primal need to protect myself and those I carried, I had used everything at my disposal.

"It still feels..." I started, but the words caught in my throat.

"I know," Maury finished softly. "It's alright for it to feel. It means you're not just a hull and engines. You have a soul, Ollie. A big, powerful, complicated one."

The sounds of the port continued around us – the steady stream of soldiers, the creak of cranes, the distant call of a ferry. The war was relentless, the next voyage always looming. But for a brief moment, sharing the burden with Maury, the terrible weight on my soul felt a fraction lighter.

"Thanks, Maury," I said, a genuine warmth spreading from my engine room to my forecastle. I just needed to... needed to say it out loud."

"Anytime, Ollie." Her presence felt like a steady anchor in the stormy sea of my memories. "We're in this together. Always have been."

I looked out at the bustling port, at the grey shape of Maury beside me, at the endless line of soldiers marching onto my decks. The ghosts were still there, the sound of the tearing metal still echoed faintly, and the faces in the water would likely never truly fade. But perhaps, the act wasn't entirely tainted. Perhaps it was just... grim necessity. Done by a ship that fought back, with every bit of power she possessed, even with the side that hadn't known the direct touch of tragedy, but fought now to ensure tragedy didn't claim anyone else. My port side. My protective side.

Chapter 18

The Overhaul

- .... . / -—...- . .- .... .- ..- .-..

The roar of the cranes overhead was a sound I hadn't truly heard in years – not like this, not with such a sense of purpose building towards future peace. It wasn't the urgent clatter of armaments being loaded or the hurried riveting of reinforcement plates. This was the clanging symphony of transformation, a shedding of the bloody grey clown suit, weary skin of war, and a reclaiming of the elegant livery I was born to wear.

I lay in drydock alongside my old friend, Mauretania, or Maury as we knew each other in the quieter moments. She too was undergoing the great unburdening, her hull being scraped free of her own crazy checkerboard, revealing patches of the proud Cunard red beneath. We weren't alone, of course. The harbour was a hive of activity, filled with ships like us, scarred veterans of the Atlantic crossing, now eager to trade depth charges for dinner gongs and troop berths for grand suites.

"Good to feel the scrapers again, isn't it, Ollie?" Maury's voice rumbled across the water, carried on the stiff breeze that snapped the flags overhead. Even in conversion, her turbines hummed with an almost impatient energy, a hint of the speed she was famous for.

"Better than feeling the sea trying to swallow you, Maury," I replied, the vibrations of the hull scraping echoing through my structure like a deep sigh. My own transformation was well underway. Inside, the cramped, functional fittings for thousands of soldiers were being ripped out, making way for the paneling, the carpets, the mirrors, the electric lights that spoke of luxury and leisure. Even my Third Class accommodations would be luxury compared to the former troop accommodations. And deeper within, a fundamental change was happening – the conversion from coal to oil.

The stokers were gone, bless their sweaty, soot-stained souls. Soon, the vast bunkers that had swallowed mountains of coal would hold liquid fuel. It meant less labour, cleaner operation, and a quieter, more consistent power. It was progress, undeniable and welcome. I felt the new pipes being laid, the tanks being fitted, a different kind of heart ready to beat within me.

"Aye," Maury agreed, her voice softening. "No more chasing bunkers in foreign ports or choking on the dust. Simple fuel pumps. It feels... cleaner in a way, doesn't it? Like washing the war out of our systems."

"Physically, perhaps," I mused, the thought catching in my metaphorical throat. "The paint, the fittings, the fuel – they change. But the memories..."

She was silent for a moment, understanding. Our conversations, when we had them in brief encounters at sea or in port, were often like this – a shared acknowledgment of what we had seen and done. We had carried so many, endured so much.

"The ghosts are harder to scrape away," Maury finished for me, her voice laced with a familiar weariness. "I still feel the weight of those boys sometimes, packed into every space, heading into the unknown. The fear... you could taste it like salt spray."

"Or the returning ones," I added, a low thrum starting deep within me, the kind that came when certain memories surfaced. "The injured. The ones who looked like the life had already been drained from them before we even reached port."

But there was one memory that pressed down on me heavier than any other. It surfaced often when I was still, when the noise of the docks faded into the background. It was the memory of the U-103.

The war had been a constant, gnawing anxiety. Every wave felt like it might conceal a periscope, every distant shadow a stalking killer. We were targets, big, tempting targets, carrying vital cargo – human lives. I had dodged, I had zig-zagged, I had relied on my escorts. I had been the 'Old Reliable', carrying quarter of a million troops across the

Atlantic without a single loss of life from enemy action. A source of pride, certainly, but built on a foundation of near-constant dread.

Still, the moment after the impact with U-103 haunted me. As I rode over him, my massive propellers continued to churn. I felt the resistance, the tearing, the violent end administered not by a gun or a torpedo, but by the very screws designed to push me gracefully through the water. And it was my port propeller, the one on the opposite side to where my sisters had been fatally wounded, that had delivered the final blow. A stark, brutal irony I could never shake. My starboard side, where I had suffered my own major injury in the Hawke collision years before, forcing me to be repaired, forcing me to change... and my port side delivering death.

Maury could apparently tell what I was thinking.

"You went after that U-boat," Maury said softly, as if sensing my thoughts drifting back to that night. "None of us were built for hunting."

"No," I agreed, the physical sensation of the impact tightening something deep inside me. "We were built for crossing. For comfort. For dreams. Not... not for that."

"But you did it," she pointed out. "You fought back. You saved your convoy."

"At what cost?" I countered, the old argument replaying in my soul. "I took a life. An enemy ship life, yes, but a life nonetheless. I was a passenger liner, Maury. I was meant to carry people to new lives, not end others."

"And if you hadn't?" she challenged gently. "How many of your troop's lives might that U-boat have taken later? How many other ships?"

It was the logical answer, the military necessity, the justification shouted in the moment of action. But logic didn't soothe the part of me that remembered the tearing steel, the unnatural feel of aggression. It felt like a violation of my very being, a betrayal of my purpose.

And then there was the other thing. The thing I carried, not just in my memory, but deep within my structure.

"It feels... complicated," I said, choosing my words carefully. "To have survived when so many didn't. To have fought back, violently, with the very parts that were meant for... for peace. And then..."

I hesitated, thinking of the massive shaft, a vital piece of my propulsion system on my starboard side. A physical link to Tinny's fate, spinning under the water, driving me forward even as she rests on the seabed.

"You mean carrying a part of Titanic?" Maury asked, her voice understanding. We ships knew these things about each other, connections that went beyond the human records in Lloyd's Register.

"Yes," I confirmed. "This starboard shaft... it was meant for her." I sighed deeply, residual smoke curling up my funnels. "They were passive victims on their starboard, and I was an active aggressor on my port, carrying a piece meant for one of the lost on my starboard."

"We carry more than cargo and passengers, don't we?" Maury said, a deep sadness in her tone. "We carry history. Their histories, our own histories. The good, the bad, the terrifying."

"The paint comes off," I said, watching as a section of my hull was revealed in its original white, gleaming dully under the shipyard lights. "The troop fittings are gone. The oil conversion will make me newer, more efficient. But the grey...' I paused, searching for the right word. 'The grey isn't just the paint, Maury. It's in here," I focused on the centre of my being, where my soul resided, intertwined with my engines, my structure, my history. "The grey is in us. The fear, the loss, the things we had to do."

"It changes you," Maury agreed. "You can't carry thousands of scared boys through submarine-infested waters for years and come out the same ship who left Liverpool with hopeful emigrants waving from the rails."

"Will we ever feel like those ships again?" I wondered aloud, the question hanging in the air between us. "The ones built for luxury, for dreams, for graceful passages?"

"We'll try," she said, her speed-loving soul revealing a quiet determination. "We'll put on the finery, light up the saloons, play the orchestras. We'll carry families on holiday, businessmen on trips, people seeking new lives. That was our purpose. We'll reclaim it."

"But we'll know," I insisted. "Every time we feel the deep water under our keel, we'll remember the fear. Every time a shadow crosses the sun, we'll think of periscopes. Every time there's a sudden lurch, we'll flinch."

"And we'll remember the ones who didn't make it," Maury added softly. "The friends lost, the sisters gone. We carry them too."

The yards were quieter than they had been during the war.

Not silent — shipyards never were — but changed. The hurried fitting of guns and troop gear had given way to restoration. Brushes moved steadily across steel, polishing cloths traced patient circles along railings, and the measured ring of tools spoke of renewal rather than urgency.

Paint replaced camouflage. Brass emerged again from beneath dull wartime coatings. Windows were uncovered, allowing light back into spaces that had long forgotten it.

We were being made into passenger ships once more.

Maury, Tania, and I rested together within one of the great salons while workers moved carefully about us. Dust sheets hung like soft curtains, and the air smelled of varnish and fresh paint instead of oil and cordite.

"It feels strange," Tania admitted quietly. "To stand still while they undo the war."

Maury gave a low hum. "Not undo," she corrected gently. "Only... cover."

I understood. The war could be repainted, but never removed.

"They restore what people remember," I said. "Not what we became."

Sunlight filtered through newly cleaned windows, falling across floors that had once held rows of bunks and wounded men. For a fleeting moment, the light moved across the polished wood in wavering patterns reflections from the harbour water outside, and I was reminded of another deck long ago, another afternoon filled with brightness before everything changed.

The feeling passed as quietly as it came.

A thrumming engine sound vibrated over the shipyard.

A smaller presence lingered there: Snowdrop.

He paused just inside the breakwater, respectful despite his youth, carrying something carefully secured.

"Olympic?" he asked, voice steady but uncertain. "Permission to come alongside?"

"You may," I answered warmly.

He approached with deliberate care, stopping before me. Maury and Tania watched with quiet curiosity.

"I was asked to find you," he said. "Carpathia told me... if I returned, this belonged with you."

He lifted what he carried: a white, weathered lifeboat assigned to Cathy, its fabric stiffened by salt and long exposure.

The shipyard seemed to grow very still.

"She held on for as long as she could," Snowdrop continued, speaking plainly, as one giving a report. "She stayed near the boats. Kept signalling. Tried to remain afloat even after the damage worsened." He hesitated briefly. "I remained with her. When the steel shark returned, I drove it off."

His voice lowered slightly.

"She was not alone at the end."

The words settled deeply within me.

I accepted the lifeboat carefully, holding it as though it carried the weight of the sea itself.

Relief came first, sharp and unexpected, followed by grief softened by gratitude.

"Thank you," I said quietly. "You have given me more comfort than you realise."

Maury inclined toward him warmly. "You performed admirable service."

Tania added, with genuine admiration, "She would have trusted you."

Snowdrop straightened slightly at that, visibly relieved that his task had been completed properly.

"I thought you should know," he said simply.

"You were right to come," I told him.

He gave a small nod, naval and precise, and withdrew, soon disappearing back into the industrious sounds of the yard.

Silence returned.

I held the lifeboat for a long while.

It was a small object, yet immense in meaning, proof of effort, of witness, of someone remaining when the sea demanded otherwise.

"She fought," Maury said softly.

"Yes," I answered. "And she was seen."

Outside, workers continued stripping away layers of wartime paint along my hull. One paused suddenly along my starboard side, calling another over in surprise.

Maury turned first. "Ollie...?"

I followed their attention.

Beneath the fading grey camouflage, revealed by careful scraping, a shallow distortion caught the light: a dent pressed deep into my plating, long hidden beneath paint.

Recognition came slowly.

A torpedo strike.

One that had failed to detonate.

I had carried the mark without knowing it.

Tania drew nearer, astonished. "You were struck… and endured."

Maury's voice softened with realization. "And it did not claim you."

For years the starboard side had carried only loss, wounds that never returned, absences that reshaped us all. Yet here was something different: damage survived. A blow delivered… and denied.

At that moment the harbour light shifted again, water reflections rippling faintly across the salon walls. For an instant, no more than a breath, the movement felt familiar, like the echo of another presence standing just beyond sight, steady and watchful as she had once been.

Not sorrowful.

Simply present.

Then the light steadied, and the moment was gone.

I looked down at the lifeboat cap resting safely in my keeping, then toward the dent revealed beside it.

Perhaps the sea had taken enough.

"It seems," Maury said gently, "the starboard side has finally chosen mercy."

Sunlight filled the salon, bright against newly restored surfaces, and for the first time since the war began, the future felt less like something to endure…

…and more like something allowed.

Chapter 19

The Interloper

- .... . / .. -. - . .-. .-. .-.. -—.—. . .-.

The tugs nudged me into position. Lines were thrown, bollards caught, and I settled into the embrace of the berth, water sighing softly against my hull. I tried to find the peace I usually felt upon returning home, but it would not come.

She, no he, loomed beside me.

Majestic.

Three great funnels rose above the dock, painted in White Star colours yet carrying a weight that felt foreign to my eye. His lines were powerful, efficient, almost blunt beside my own familiar grace. All size and certainty, occupying a space that once belonged to Britt.

I felt his awareness turn toward me.

Protocol demanded courtesy.

"Good afternoon," I projected across the narrow water. "A fine day for port."

"Good afternoon, Olympic," came the reply, calm and measured. "You've arrived from New York?"

"Indeed. A straightforward crossing."

Silence followed — thick with things unsaid.

I could not hold them back.

"It is still... strange," I admitted. "Seeing you here. In our colours."

He did not respond immediately.

"You are the replacement," I continued, the words sharpening despite myself. "Britannic was family. Built here. One of us. And you... you were built by the very nation that brought so much loss."

The dock noises seemed to fade.

He absorbed the words without protest.

"I understand why you would feel that way," he began quietly.

But before he could continue, another presence entered the harbour.

Maury.

She approached with purpose, and beside her came two immense liners I knew well by reputation but had rarely seen together.

Berengaria, or Bernie, elegant despite his size.

And Leviathan, or Levi, broad, confident, carrying an unmistakable American energy.

The moment they drew near, everything changed.

"Jesse!" Levi boomed, his voice bright with relief. "Well I'll be! Look at you! All finished and floatin'. Took 'em long enough, didn't it?"

Bernie's tone followed, warm but composed. "Ach, mein Bruder... at last. Whole. Sailing properly. It is good to see you alive in the world."

Majestic seemed almost smaller beside their affection, though nothing about him physically changed.

"You made it," Maury added gently, pride evident.

I hesitated, caught off guard. This was not how one greeted an enemy vessel.

Levi turned toward me, noticing my confusion.

"Oh, Ollie, right? Yeah, you probably only heard the official story." He gave a low whistle. "That version skips a whole lotta misery."

Bernie inclined slightly toward me, voice measured and precise.

"He was never truly theirs, you understand. Not in the end. When the war began, he stood unfinished, only a shell. A promise without life."

Levi nodded. "Yeah. Big guy sat there for years like an empty warehouse. They stripped him clean. Pipes, copper, fittings, anything they could melt down for shells. Didn't matter that he wasn't even born yet."

A faint vibration passed through Majestic, but he said nothing.

Bernie continued softly, choosing each word carefully.

"They dismantled parts of him before he ever sailed. Imagine being undone before becoming."

I felt an uneasy chill through my plates.

"And when the war ended," Levi added, "nobody wanted to finish him. Too expensive. Too complicated. Just sat there rustin' while everyone argued what to do."

Bernie's voice lowered.

"Then came the treaty. He was not chosen. He was given away. Like property."

Levi snorted. "And just when they finally start fixin' him up again: boom. Fire in the yard. Nearly cooked him before he even saw water."

A fire. I understood fire.

Bernie nodded solemnly. "Sabotage, they said. Anger from those who watched him taken. He suffered for a war he never fought."

Levi folded in the final piece, voice quieter now.

"Then your people came. New crew aboard one side, old crew marched off the other. No goodbyes. Just... swap and go."

The image struck harder than any accusation.

"They painted over his name," Bernie said gently. "Changed his purpose. Changed his home."

Levi shrugged. "Guy didn't even get a say in what he was called. One day Bismarck, next day Majestic. That's a rough identity switch, sister."

Silence settled over us.

I looked at Jesse again, truly looked. Not a conqueror. Not a replacement. A survivor reshaped by forces he never chose.

He finally spoke, voice quiet. "I did not come here to take anyone's place." The words carried no defense. Only fact.

Something inside me shifted.

All this time I had seen him as the symbol of victory, a prize imposed upon us.

But he had not arrived triumphant. He had arrived displaced.

War had taken my sisters.

War had taken his very beginning.

History, I realized slowly, was not divided as neatly as we wished, not into builders and destroyers, victors and enemies. Steel remembered differently.

"My dear…" I said at last, my tone softer than it had been in years. "You have had a truly ghastly time of it."

Levi gave a small approving hum. Bernie smiled faintly.

Majestic inclined his bow slightly.

"It has been… complicated."

I studied him a moment longer, then allowed a hint of warmth into my voice.

"Well," I said, almost casually, "if you are to remain among us… we cannot go about calling you 'Majestic' all the time. Far too formal."

A pause.

"How does… Jesse sound?"

Levi laughed outright. "Kid finally gets a proper nickname."

Bernie nodded approvingly. "Ja. It suits him."

And for the first time since docking, the harbour felt a little less crowded by ghosts.

The harbour gradually returned to its ordinary rhythm. Cargo cranes resumed their steady groan, gulls circled overhead, and the excitement of reunion softened into quiet conversation among the others.

Maury drifted closer beside me, her presence warm but thoughtful.

"Well," she said at last, a faint note of amusement beneath her usual composure, "that went differently than I expected."

I gave a small, self-conscious hum. "You expected me to be less… accommodating?"

"I expected you to hold your ground longer," she admitted gently. "You have guarded your sisters' memory fiercely since the war. I thought you might see him only as an intrusion."

I watched Jesse speaking quietly with Bernie and Levi, their easy familiarity already forming a circle around him that felt strangely natural.

"I did," I confessed. "At first."

Maury waited, sensing there was more.

"For so long," I continued, "I believed acceptance meant forgetting. That allowing someone new beside us diminished those we lost." I paused, considering the thought as I spoke it aloud. "But listening to them... I realised he did not arrive here by triumph. He arrived carrying his own scars."

Maury's funnels gave a thoughtful vibration. "War rarely leaves anyone untouched."

"No," I agreed softly. "And I would not be a proper White Star liner if I could not recognise endurance when I see it."

She turned slightly toward me, curious.

"We were built to carry people forward," I said. "Not to hold the past so tightly that nothing new may come aboard."

For a moment Maury said nothing. Then a quiet warmth entered her tone.

"Tinny would have approved of that," she said.

The words settled gently between us.

"I hope so," I replied.

We stood together in companionable silence, watching as Jesse laughed awkwardly at something Levi said, the sound tentative, as though he were still learning how to belong.

And for the first time since his arrival, I no longer felt as though a space had been taken.

Only that another survivor had found harbour.

Chapter 20

The Friend

- .... . / ..-. .-. .. . -. -..

Ah, New York! The salty tang of the Atlantic mingling with the grimy breath of the city, the cacophony of dockworkers, hooting tugs, and rattling carts – it was a symphony I knew well. My mooring lines were secured at my usual berth, the grand Hudson River stretching out before me under a sky the colour of faded denim. It was the year 1922, and I felt the familiar thrum deep within my steel plating. I was loading up again, preparing for the eastward run to Southampton, a task I had performed countless times before, yet one that always felt significant. There was a comforting rhythm to it – the rumble of cargo being stowed, the laughter of passengers boarding, the anticipation of the open sea.

I watched Berengaria, Bernie, as Maury had taken to calling him, settle into his berth. He carried himself with a quiet elegance despite his immense size, his lines familiar now after several shared seasons upon the Atlantic. We had crossed paths before in passing ports and distant anchorages, exchanging only brief courtesies. Today, however, circumstance granted us time.

I sent a polite greeting across the water.

"Welcome back to New York, Bernie. I trust the crossing treated you kindly?"

There was only a brief pause before his reply came, warm and recognizably familiar.

"Lady Olympic. Ja, it was a good voyage. The sea behaved itself for once. I am glad to see you again."

The German cadence remained in his speech, softened now by years of Atlantic service but never entirely gone.

"One always appreciates cooperative weather," I replied. "Particularly after the years we have known."

"Ach, yes," he agreed quietly. "Calm seas feel... earned now."

I felt my earlier reserve ease. There was steadiness in him: not bravado, not rivalry, simply presence.

"Maury speaks well of you," I said. "She seems to have taken you thoroughly under her wing."

A faint warmth entered his tone. "She has been very patient with me. The Atlantic trade has its own manners, its own expectations. I am still learning them, though she insists I improve."

That sounded very much like Maury.

"She worries more than she admits," I said.

"I have noticed," Bernie replied gently. "Especially when speaking of Lusitania."

His voice lowered respectfully.

"That loss... it remains close to her."

"As do my own," I answered quietly.

He hesitated a moment, then continued with careful sincerity.

"She told me of Titanic. And Britannic. I wished to say... you have my deepest sympathy, Olympic. Such absences do not diminish with time."

It was strange: once I might have resisted comfort from a ship built under another flag. Now it felt natural.

"Thank you, Bernie. They were remarkable ships."

A brief silence passed before he spoke again.

"And... he told me also of your encounter with the U-boat."

"I did what necessity required," I said evenly.

"Ja," Bernie replied, and for the first time a firm edge entered his voice. "Those weapons brought dishonour to many who never chose such warfare. Merchant ships were not meant for such hunting."

The conviction surprised me, not anger, but moral clarity.

"You were laid up during those years," I prompted gently.

A deep resonance passed through him, heavy with memory.

"Laid up," he repeated. "That is a polite description. I was unfinished... and forgotten. Years in harbour without purpose. Watching others sail while I remained still." He paused. "For a ship, inactivity is a slow unmaking."

I understood that instinctively.

"A ship requires motion," I said.

"Exactly," he answered softly. "Then, after the Armistice, everything changed. Suddenly I was needed, not for pride, but for return. I carried thousands of American soldiers home. So many... tired, relieved, alive." A quiet pride entered his voice. "It was chaos, but meaningful chaos. For the first time, I felt I had justified my existence."

"A noble service," I said sincerely.

He seemed pleased by that acknowledgment.

"And now," he continued, "I sail with Cunard. Maury guides me well. And my captain... is Sir Arthur Rostron."

The name settled heavily between us.

Sir Arthur Rostron.

"I know him," I said quietly. "A remarkable man."

"Ja," Bernie replied warmly. "He understands responsibility. He speaks often of vigilance... and compassion. The crew trusts him completely."

Images stirred within memory: cold waters, distant lights, salvation arriving through darkness.

"He has earned that trust," I said.

Bernie continued, more thoughtfully now.

"When Maury spoke of Lusitania... and when I learned of your sisters... I understood something. I cannot replace what was lost. No ship can. But perhaps..." he paused, choosing his words carefully, "...perhaps I may honour them by sailing well. By being worthy of the space I now occupy."

His sentiment resonated deeply.

"That is all any of us may do," I told him. "We carry forward what cannot return."

He seemed to settle at that.

"I am glad you understand," he said quietly. "History is often described in simple opposites. But ships... we endure consequences, not intentions."

"Well said," I replied.

I thought then of Jessie, my Majestic, and the difficult path that had brought her into our family.

"I have learned something similar myself," I added. "My Majestic came to us with a complicated past. Acceptance was... necessary for both of us."

Bernie's tone brightened gently. "Ja, Maury told me you gave him a nickname. Jesse, yes? That was a kindness."

"It seemed appropriate," I said. "He had lost enough without losing belonging as well."

There was a soft pause.

"You are kinder than your reputation suggests, Olympic," Bernie said with quiet amusement.

"I prefer to think I am practical," I replied.

He laughed softly, a restrained, dignified sound.

"It is good," he said, "that ships like us continue to sail together."

"It is," I agreed. "We understand one another in ways few others can."

The evening light lengthened across the docks as activity slowed.

"Well then, Bernie," I said at last, "it is good to see you again. And comforting to know Maury has such steady company."

"The feeling is mutual, Ollie," he replied warmly. "May our courses cross often."

"Safe voyages."

"And to you."

Log Entry — RMS Olympic

Private Master's Log — Supplemental Entry

Southampton Water

Evening Watch, alongside

Voyage completed as scheduled.

Westbound and return passages conducted under generally favourable conditions. Moderate Atlantic swell encountered mid-crossing; no incidents of consequence recorded. Passengers conveyed safely and in good order. Docking effected without difficulty. Engines secured at 18:40 hours.

Routine restored.

There was a period when such entries could not be written with certainty. During the war years each sailing carried unknown variables: altered courses, darkened horizons, vigilance maintained without pause. The sea felt narrower then, though no chart recorded the change.

It has widened again.

Passenger traffic increases steadily. Families and travellers now occupy spaces once given to troops and hospital berths. Music has returned to the saloons. Deck chairs line the promenades where watch stations once stood. The sounds are different now: lighter, though not forgotten.

Many familiar vessels continue in service. Mauretania maintains her admirable speed and bearing. Berengaria and Leviathan have settled into regular crossings with confidence. Majestic, Jesse as he is more commonly known among us, sails well and carries himself with quiet assurance. Time and shared duty have rendered former distinctions less significant than once believed.

The Atlantic remains unchanged in its nature, yet altered in memory.

Certain absences are still noted during early watches and in heavy fog, when visibility shortens and distance plays its old tricks.

Experience suggests these impressions pass with steady course and sufficient light.

Operations continue as expected. Crew performance satisfactory. Hull and machinery responding reliably following refit improvements. Endurance remains adequate for present service demands.

It is a comfort to record uneventful passages once more.

Orders received for next sailing. Coaling to commence at first light. Preparations underway.

Sea and ship in good condition.

All secure.

— Olympic

Also by Charles Bates

Ravenheart and a Feather: Sisters of the Deep
Veteran Queens: If These Hulls Could Talk
Commissioned